Power Trip 2

Power Trip 2

Treasure Malian

www.urbanbooks.net

Urban Books, LLC
300 Farmingdale Road, NY-Route 109
Farmingdale, NY 11735

ISBN 13: 978-1-64556-023-4
ISBN 10: 1-64556-023-6

First Trade Paperback Printing June 2020
Printed in the United States of America

10 9 8 7 6 5 4 3 2 1

Distributed by Kensington Publishing Corp.
Submit Orders to:
Customer Service
400 Hahn Road
Westminster, MD 21157-4627
Phone: 1-800-733-3000
Fax: 1-800-659-2436

Power Trip 2

by

Treasure Malian

Cast of Characters

Ariana: Long-time best friend of Skye. Their relations turned sour once Ariana withheld information from Skye and Cameron about the guy, Man, she was seeing, who was at odds with Cameron, which resulted in Cameron being shot. After details about her dealings with Man emerged, Skye wanted her dead. In response to that, Ariana kidnapped Skye's son, Cairo.

Skye: Girlfriend of Cameron, who took over his drug empire after he had been shot with the help of her grandfather, Pop Pop, and Cameron's best friend, Ty.

Ty: Cameron's best friend and underboss. Ex-boyfriend to Ariana and current love interest of Cameron's little sister, Victoria.

Man: Opposition responsible for shooting Cameron.

Chapter One

Ariana

I wasn't going to sit around and listen to Ty threaten me. I knew that he took my demand seriously because I already went this far. I didn't need to prove anything else for the moment. I pressed end call and put the phone down beside me. I focused my attention back on the screaming Cairo. I guessed he sensed that I wasn't his mother, because he cried almost nonstop since we'd gotten to New York. He barely allowed me to touch him, which made it almost impossible for me to feed him. In no way was it my intention to hurt him. I needed results, and I knew that having Cairo would guarantee that. All that was left for me to do was figure out how I could receive what I want, return Cairo, and keep my life. Until I had a solid plan in place, Cairo would stay in my possession. He was my insurance.

He needed to eat and have some uninterrupted sleep, but it just wasn't happening with me. That's when it hit me. I picked up my phone and called the only person in the world who would be able to help me. I tried to drown out Cairo's cries as I listened to the phone ring, hoping that she would answer.

"Hello, daughter, it's nice of you to finally decide to call me. I just finish talking to Ty. He's such a nice boy," she said as she answered the phone.

I was wrong for keeping my mother out of the loop, but at the time, it was the only card I had to play. I was supposed to be a dead woman, and no one would have believed that for a minute if my mother was her normal upbeat self. I didn't go so far as making her think I was dead too, but I did keep my distance, having her worry about my well-being. I had to stay off the grid for a while. I knew Ty would call there asking for me.

"I'm sorry about that. You know how things have been with Skye. I've just been helping her out. Please don't tell Ty you spoke to me. We are still broken up. I'm trying to sort through that without him hounding me." I felt bad lying to her, but sometimes you had to tell a little white lie to protect a much bigger issue.

"You don't have to worry. Your momma knows how that go. How is Skye? And who is that crying like that?" she said, biting the bait just as I expected her to.

"She's hanging in there, Mom, and that's Cairo. He's here spending some time with his godmother and giving Skye a break." I let the lies flow effortlessly, hoping that she would believe them.

"That's really nice of you. Please bring him over, because I haven't even gotten to see a picture of him," she said with sadness in her tone.

She was hurt about the way things had gone down with her and Adriana a few years back, causing a rift in their friendship. My mom tried to push up on Skye's dad, and Adriana lost it. I couldn't really blame her. Because of that, my mother avoided all things related to Adriana, which was why I knew taking Cairo to her house wouldn't pose any threats to my plans. She definitely wouldn't be calling Adriana. Skye wouldn't call my mother either, since I was supposed to be dead. Ty wasn't dumb enough to reveal his failure because he was going to handle this situation on his own. That I knew for a fact. He would never want to risk being seen as untrustworthy to Cam or Skye. My plan was foolproof.

"Okay, Mom, once he settles down, I'll bring him by," I replied, doing backflips in my head.

We spoke for a little while longer before ending the call. I wasn't going to sit around and wait for Cairo to settle, because that would never happen. It wasn't like the nights before when he would just cry himself to sleep. I grabbed his bag and picked him up off the bed before heading out to catch a taxi.

I stood in front of the Marriott located in downtown Brooklyn, and I flagged down a cab. As I slid into the back seat of the taxi, the cool air from the air conditioning hit me, and I let out a sigh of relief. The heat was no joke. We were no more than five minutes into the ride when Cairo drifted off to sleep. I completely forgot that Ty mentioned car rides put him to sleep. I would have used this method to get some peace and quiet. For the duration of the ride, I stared out the window, thinking about my next move. If you would have ever told me things would be this way between Skye and me, I would have laughed in your face. I shook my head, thinking about all the events that had occurred this past year.

As the cab came to a stop in front of my mother's brownstone, I pulled out a $20 bill and handed it to the driver. Usually I was the type to say, "Keep the change," but times had changed. That change was much needed for my next meal. I was jobless, and Ty wasn't fronting my bill anymore. The cash I did have left I had to stretch until he came through with what I'd asked for.

When he handed me back my change, I stuffed it down into the front pocket of my denim Old Navy shorts. As my Chuck Taylors hit the pavement, I chuckled to myself at how my life had changed. Although there was nothing funny about it, I had to laugh to keep from crying. There

I was parading around in Old Navy and Chucks. Don't get me wrong, there was nothing wrong with either for anyone else. It just wasn't my style. It was nothing that I was willing to get used to.

I staggered up the steps with Cairo sleeping over my right shoulder and his bag slung across the left. I rang the doorbell and waited patiently for an answer. Moments later, my mother opened the door and instantly reached for Cairo, which was definitely a relief.

Once we were inside the house, my mother and I sat in the living room and caught up. Of course, my version of what I had been up to was completely fabricated as I couldn't come out and tell her the truth about what had been going on. There was no way I could find the words to explain to her that I kidnapped Cairo to get revenge on Skye, who wanted me dead. Maybe the words would come, but I definitely wouldn't be able to convince her to see things my way, so I didn't bother. We talked for a minute until Cairo woke up. I automatically expected him to go into one of his crying fits, but instead, he smiled at my mother as she cooed over him.

I took that as an opportunity to slip away and call my boo. I hadn't seen him in weeks. Receiving his pipe was long overdue. I thought about his immaculate sex game as I walked out of the living room toward the kitchen and called his phone.

"What up, Ari?" he spoke as he answered.

"I just got in the crib from visiting my mom's and shit. About to chill. Nothing major," he replied.

"I want to see you. Can you come get me from my mother's house?" I asked, hoping that he would come.

"Text me the address. I'll be out there soon," he said.

I could hear the smile on his face. He must have had the same plans I did. "Okay, I can't wait to see you," I said before hanging up the phone.

I looked down at the phone and saw a text pop up from Man.

Yo, Ari, what up? I need to see you, shorty.

Completely ignoring his text, I texted my boo the address and headed back into the living room to wait for him with my mother and Cairo.

Skye

I lay in bed, tossing and turning, racking my brain, trying to figure out who had anything to gain from taking Cairo, but I continued to come up short. I sat up and tossed one of my pillows to the floor and let out an exasperated sigh. I was frustrated. It would have been much easier if I knew where he was so I could put a plan together to get him back. The unknown was killing me. I just wanted my baby. It had been a week, I hadn't had a proper meal or an adequate amount of sleep, and it was beginning to take its toll on me. I hadn't realized how weak I was until I tried to stand up. Feeling the gravity pull me down toward the floor, I sat back on the bed.

The knocking at my door grabbed my attention. "Come in," I called out with an inkling of energy.

"Hey, sis. Come downstairs and eat. I don't want to hear that you're not hungry. You gotta put something in your system." Victoria said in a sincere tone.

I didn't budge. I understood her concern. It was valid, but I didn't care. Until someone in that house understood how it felt to not know where their child was or if their child was okay, I didn't want to hear anything. No one knew the pain and void I was feeling. It was worse than not knowing if Cameron would make it. Yes, I'd been hurting during that time, but this was my son. The pain was incomparable.

I watched as Victoria walked toward me, taking slow strides. I knew she was being cautious since, as of late, I'd been snapping on everyone. She needed not to worry at that moment, because I just didn't have the energy. She took a seat on the bed next to me and draped her arm over my shoulder. Unconsciously I leaned my head against hers and wept.

"I want my son, Victoria," I cried out.

She said nothing. There wasn't anything she could say to console me, and she knew that. Instead, she rubbed my back while I cried, causing my tears to form a pool on the pillow that rested on my lap. My phone started to ring, causing both Victoria and me to stiffen. We stared at each other for a split second before Victoria pulled the charger out of the base of the phone and lifted it from the nightstand.

She glanced down, and her shoulders dropped in disappointment. "It's Ty," she said as she slid her finger across the screen to answer. "Hey, babe," she spoke softly into the phone.

She listened attentively before sticking her hand out to give me the phone. I sat still for a moment, not really wanting to talk. I owed it to Ty to take his calls regardless of my mood, so I reached for the phone and pressed it against my cheek.

"Yes," I said to alert him that I now had the phone.

"Sis, I don't know how to tell you this . . ." he began, but his choice of words sent me into panic mode.

"No, Ty! Unless you are telling me that you found my son unharmed and are bringing him back to me, I don't want to hear it. Anything else would be totally fucking unacceptable!" I barked into the phone, not meaning to take my frustration and anger out on him. I just couldn't bear bad news about my son.

"Sis, hear me out, please," Ty spoke in a soothing tone, trying to calm me down.

The only thing that calmed me down was not hearing panic in his voice. I knew how much Ty loved Cairo, and if he was about to deliver bad news, devastation would surely ooze through his tone. It didn't.

"What happened?" I was growing impatient. I needed him to get to the point and get there fast.

"Ariana has him," Ty said after taking a deep breath.

I didn't hear him clearly. I couldn't have. "Who?" I asked for reassurance that I had indeed heard him correctly.

"Ari . . ." he reiterated.

Time froze, or at least it felt that way. The steady beat of my heart gradually increased as a million and one thoughts rushed through my mind. I wanted to scream and curse Ty out, but what good would that have done? I still needed to get my son back.

"I'm on my way," I said as I pressed end on my phone.

"What happened?" Victoria asked.

Having the first real lead since Cairo was taken, I felt optimistic. I would have to deal with Ty's indiscretion, but it had to go on the back burner until Cairo was back safe with me, where he belonged. I stood and walked over to my closet, completely ignoring Victoria's question. I didn't know how serious she and Ty had gotten, so I wasn't ready to disclose to her what he'd told me until I had the facts.

"What happened?" Victoria asked again, this time walking up to me as I stood in my closet in search of something to wear.

"I'm going home," I replied nonchalantly.

"I'm going with you," she said as she turned on her heels and walked out of the room.

There was no point in arguing with her. Once Victoria set her mind on doing something, that's exactly what she was going to do. I was seeing more similarities between her and Cameron as the days went on.

As I slipped into the True Religion shorts and True T-shirt I'd snatched out of the closet, my mind floated back to Ty. I still couldn't wrap my brain around the thought of him not completing the one thing I desperately needed him to do. A part of me wanted to blame him for Cairo's kidnapping, but then again, even if Ty didn't do what I asked, Ariana had taken it to another level by bringing my son into this shit. He would definitely have to deal with me, but at the top of my list was getting my baby back and personally handling Ariana like I should have done when we first found out she'd been fucking with the nigga Man.

Once I was completely dressed, I grabbed the Chanel bag that was sitting on my chaise and quickly browsed through it, making sure it held my necessities. Satisfied that everything I needed was in there, I set out to find Victoria and get on the first thing smoking back to New York.

Cameron

Vic just finished telling me that Ty called with a lead on Cairo. I was trying to understand why my right-hand nigga didn't reach out to me first. In their eyes, I was just some handicap-ass nigga who wasn't capable of getting shit done, and that was pissing me off. Niggas felt like my attitude and how I'd been acting was unnecessary, but none of them knew how this shit felt. None of them knew how useless a nigga felt. I even had to cut my showers short because a nigga couldn't stand for a certain amount of time before feeling like my fucking legs were going to cave in. This shit was frustrating, to say the least.

I wanted to hunt and gun down whoever was responsible for taking my son, and it was killing me that I couldn't. I felt like less of a man, not being able to step up and handle shit. Handling shit had always been my thing. Even before my pops got killed, I was the man of the house. I felt like shit, and to make matters worse, my girl had to be the man. As time passed, I was supposed to start feeling better, but as my body got better physically, I was suffering emotionally.

"Victoriaaaaa!" I heard Skye call out.

Hearing her voice made me wanna flip the fuck out. Why couldn't shit be the way it was a few months back? Shit was sweet. I had my girl, and we were good.

"I'm in the living room," Vic shouted back.

"I was looking for you. You ready?" Skye said as she walked into the living room.

"Yeah, I was just talking to Cam," Vic said as she stood to leave.

"You not going to tell me where you going? Or tell your mother for that matter?" I asked her, wondering why she was acting as if I weren't present.

Ty

Delivering that news to Skye was one of the worst things I'd had to do to date, and I'd done some fucked-up shit. She was family, and the last thing I wanted was for her to hurt. She didn't deserve it. She had been through enough that past year. I knew that I could have gotten Cairo back on my own, but there'd already been too many secrets. Skye deserved to know the minute I found out it was my fault, so I owed her that much at least.

I really wasn't ready to face her or Cameron because I knew I would have to answer for the shit I did. I just hoped shit wouldn't be too sour. All depended on whether we got Cairo back. I wasn't too worried about that part because I had every intention of getting my godson back. I didn't care who had to be bodied. Cairo was going to be returned to Skye and Cam. I would die making sure that happened.

I called and texted everybody I knew who knew Ariana, and I felt confident that someone would hit me back with news that would help me find her. Even better if they would hit me with her exact location. At that point, though, any bit of information would have been useful. In the meantime, there wasn't shit for me to do except wait for Skye to touch down or one of my niggas to get at me, whichever came first.

I kicked my feet up on the coffee table just as my phone started ringing. I picked it up off the seat beside me and saw that it was a text from Skye.

Be at JFK at 6:30.

I glanced at the time on my Hublot and saw that I had a few hours to burn before I needed to be at the airport. I set the alarm on my phone and turned up the volume before lying back on the couch with my eyes closed. Since Cairo was taken, sleep had been the furthest thing from my mind. But now that we were a step closer to getting him back, I figured I could snatch some z's until it was go time.

The alarm blared throughout the house, awakening me from my power nap and signaling that it was time for me to head to the airport. I stretched before picking up my phone and going through my text messages.

"Fuck!" I yelled in frustration.

Not one text with info on that bitch's whereabouts. I knew I needed to be patient, but time wasn't on my side. I headed into the bathroom and quickly washed my face and brushed my teeth before dipping out and heading to the airport.

I pulled up to the airport at six thirty on the nose and sent Skye a text letting her know I was there and waiting for her.

> *You'd take the clothes off my back, and I'd let you*
> *You'd steal the food right out my mouth*
> *And I'd watch you eat it*

Hearing Hov's "Holy Grail" track coming through the car speakers, I reached for the volume and turned it up. I didn't really fuck with the nigga Justin Timberlake, but the song was fire. It didn't matter what track it was. If it was Hov, a nigga fucked with it. That was the Brooklyn nigga in me.

Hov was rapping about having tats and psycho bitches by the time I spotted Skye and Victoria headed toward the car. "Fuck, I gotta deal with Vic too," I said out loud just as they opened the back doors and climbed in the truck. "What up, y'all?" I said as I turned the key in the ignition.

"Hey, babe," Vic said.

I glanced back as Skye put her ear buds in and sat back with her eyes closed. She was pissed off with me for not handling Ariana, and I couldn't even blame her. Only way I could have even begun to mend our friendship was by getting her son back. Until that happened, there wouldn't be any talking to her. I let out a sigh as I pulled off and headed back to Skye's crib.

Skye

When we got to my place, I wanted to jump right into the search for Cairo and Ariana. I wasn't in the mood to waste any time. I definitely wasn't going to waste it talking.

"What information you got for me?" I asked Ty as soon as we walked through the door. I didn't give him the chance to settle in, and I didn't care. Fuck how he felt, and fuck him being comfortable! If he had done what was asked of him, we wouldn't even be here.

"Nothing. I hit up everybody who would possibly have information or who I knew could get information. Just gotta wait it out now," he said, causing me to cock my head to the side and stare at him oddly.

"Wait it out? Nah, that's not how this is going to work. I'm not about to sit around and wait for people to get back to you with information while this crazy bitch does only God knows what with my son. That's just not going to work for me," I said, hoping he understood that I meant I wanted his feet and ears to the street.

"Crazy bitch. Wait, I'm so lost. Who has Cairo?" Victoria asked, looking back and forth from me to Ty and back to me.

"Care to share, Ty?" I said, walking into the living room.

"Babe . . ." Ty started to explain.

I just hated when niggas fucked up and thought they would be able to make it better by starting off their excuse with "babe." Females weren't dumb. I knew for sure Victoria wasn't.

"Nah, don't babe me. Who has my nephew?" she asked again, this time raising her voice.

"Ariana," Ty said in barely a whisper.

The loud thud was what caught my attention. I turned around to Ty rubbing the side of his face. I automatically knew the sound I'd heard was Victoria's fist colliding with his face.

"The fuck you mean, a dead bitch has my nephew?" she screamed, swinging on him again.

I jumped in between them because I didn't want Ty to hit her back. If he did, we would have had to kill him before getting Cairo back, and I needed his resources.

"Victoria, calm down," I said while pushing her back into the foyer and away from Ty.

"No! Ain't no calm down. He was supposed to kill that bitch because she made the choice to keep her knowing Man a secret from us, causing all this shit. Now she has my nephew. Ty, on my pop's grave, if we don't get Cairo back, I'ma body you." She screamed out the promise.

Ty probably took it as an idle threat, but I knew better. She was her father's daughter and her brother's Mini-Me. If pushed, it would definitely be slow singing and flower bringing for Ty.

I continued to try to calm her down, but my efforts were in vain as she continued to rant and curse Ty out. I understood because I wanted to do the same exact thing, except I knew I had to stay level-headed and focused on the most important goal to me, which was getting my baby.

"What, you was fucking that bitch still, Ty? Keep it a rack. You had to be fucking her. There's no other reason why you would cross us like this. I expected so much more from you." Victoria was mad and hurt.

That moment when she broke down in tears, I really realized how much feeling she really had for Ty. I thought he noticed it too. He tried to get closer to console her, but I pushed him back.

"Give her space," I said, trying to keep a decent distance between them.

"It wasn't like that. I wasn't fucking her. When I went to her crib, I had every intention of killing her," he started to explain.

Although it didn't matter, I was curious. I really did want to know what in his right mind made him leave that trifling bitch breathing. "Then why?" I asked him.

"It happened so fast. I didn't really have the chance to process it. I just reacted. I was ready to send her to meet her Maker when she told me that the night she got shot, she miscarried my baby. I couldn't kill her. I wanted to. On everything, I really did want to body shorty. I just couldn't do it. She lost my seed. On top of that, it was my fault. I took her to the club that night. She should have been home with you, but I had her in the fucking strip club.

"Vic, I swear I ain't have no feelings for Ari. I wasn't fucking her, wasn't thinking about fucking her, or nothing. That shit just fucked me up. So I let her go. I told her to get low because next time she wouldn't be lucky. I really didn't think she would turn around and do some crazy shit like this, man."

As he spoke, I stared at him intently, searching for a lie or one hint of bullshit. There was none. I didn't sympathize with Ariana, because her losing a child shouldn't have driven her to bring my son into our beef. But no matter how much I wanted to hate Ty, in that instant, I couldn't.

I totally understood. I was a mother. Yes, my son went full term, but every day during my pregnancy, I worried that stress would take him from me. If those thoughts had become my reality, I wouldn't have been able to go on living, so I completely understood and sympathized with that.

"I'm sorry, sis. You know I love Cai as if the little nigga were my own. I would never want him in no shit like this. I know it's my fault, and I'm ready to do whatever needs to be done to make it right," he proceeded to apologize.

Ty was never one to bullshit, so I took his words to heart and for what they were. "I forgive you. Believe it or not, I understand. My main focus right now is getting my son back, that's all. Nothing else matters to me," I said, walking away and leaving Ty and Victoria in the foyer alone.

I hoped that they wouldn't come to blows, but I needed a breather.

Victoria

I understood why Skye wanted to forgive Ty, but I wouldn't give in that easy. *He better hope that we get my nephew back unharmed.* That's the only way I would even consider letting him see another day. I stared at him for a minute before he decided to take a step closer to me. I moved back and put up my hand, signaling him not to move.

"I have nothing to say to you." I walked around him toward the back of the house where Skye had gone. Her door was open, so I walked in without knocking. I found her sitting on the chaise in front of her window, staring out at nothing in particular.

"You okay?" I asked as I took a seat next to her.

"I will be when I get my son. I really hope she doesn't hurt my baby. Cairo doesn't deserve to be caught up in my mess. I pray God keeps him safe until I can get him back." She spoke softly, on the verge of tears.

"We will get him back," I said, trying to reassure her.

She didn't respond. Instead, she continued to stare off as if I weren't present. There was nothing I could really say to make her feel any better. I couldn't relate, either. Yeah, I was hurting and wanted my nephew home safe and sound, but she was his mother. Her heart had to be on a different level.

She wouldn't hurt for long, though. Not if I could help it. I wasn't going to stop until we got the baby back. Nothing would save Ariana from the pain I planned to inflict on her once I got my hands on her. At that moment, though, we didn't have any leads on Ariana's whereabouts, so all we could do was patiently wait it out. Information would come, and when it did, we would be ready.

Chapter Two

Ariana

My baby came and picked me up from my mother's house as promised. I was just thankful that she didn't protest when I asked her to watch Cairo for a few hours. If it were up to me, it would have been days before I went back to get him. He just cried too much, plus he would be safe with my mother.

"Shorty, you hungry?" His smooth voice brought me out of my own head.

I looked up to him and smiled. "Nah, babe, I'm good for the moment."

Grabbing the remote, he sat down on the couch next to me and started flipping through the channels. I leaned over and rested my head on his shoulder and thought back to when we first started kicking it.

When I first met him, I wasn't attracted to him in the least. It wasn't because he wasn't cute, because he was. He had smooth chocolate skin, which I absolutely loved, shoulder-length dreads that were always neat, almond-shaped brown eyes that had a hint of mystery behind them, and he was built. I just couldn't focus too much on how good-looking he was because, at that time, Ty and I were kicking it hard. I wasn't checking for nobody but him, especially nobody on his own team. Yeah, I still messed with Man from time to time, but that was different. Man and I had history. It wouldn't be easy to give him up. Definitely couldn't do it cold turkey.

Every time I was around him, he would be extra friendly and shit, but I didn't pay it any attention. I thought he was on some brother-sister shit because that was how it was with everyone on the team. However, those thoughts changed on the first day he came to the hospital to see me after I got shot.

"How you feeling?" he said as he walked in the room with flowers and a "get well soon" card.

"I mean, I have been better, but I'm alive, so no complaining about that," I replied, smiling.

"That's good. Where your man?" he asked in reference to Ty.

"You probably would know better than me. I haven't seen him in a few days. I guess he's been busy," I said, looking down and trying to avoid eye contact. I didn't want him to see how hurt I was that Ty wasn't there.

"If you were my girl, I wouldn't leave you alone in here for a minute. These niggas would have had to put me out," he said, taking a seat next to my bed and rubbing my hand.

Skye

I woke up to the sun peeking through my window. I had no idea that I'd even fallen asleep. I couldn't deny that the sleep was much needed. I glanced at the cable box, and the bright neon numbers read 9:43 a.m. I sat up in bed and took a few deep breaths before swinging my legs over and planting them both on the floor. I stood up and stretched my five foot three inch frame as high as it could go before heading into the bathroom to wash my face and brush my teeth.

I stared in the mirror at my reflection and nearly cringed. It wasn't because I was ugly or had any signs of wear and tear on my exterior, but because I felt ugly inside. Somewhere along the way, I lost sight of who Skye was. I was warned that this would happen, but I thought I had everything under control and continued to do what I wanted, disregarding the warnings. Now there I was. If I was going to be able to put my life back in order, I needed to start right away. I planned on it, but not until I got my baby boy and Ariana was taking a dirt nap.

I turned on the shower and peeled the previous day's clothes off my body before stepping in. The water massage was feeling really good and was much needed. I stood directly under the showerhead and allowed the water to beat down on me like the jets in the Jacuzzi tub at Cameron's house, which I absolutely loved. I lathered Dove body wash in my sponge and proceeded to wash my tired body.

After the shower, I slipped into a pair of Victoria's Secret PINK sweats and a PINK T-shirt. Not really a typical outfit for me, but I didn't really care. I didn't have anyone to impress. As I turned the knob to my bedroom door to join Ty and Victoria, it hit me. I skipped back over to my bed and took a seat as I unplugged my cell phone from the charger. I scrolled through the phone book in search of the person who I prayed would have the answers that I desperately needed.

As I listened to the phone ring, I felt my heart rate increase as well as the beating of my heart against my chest walls. The moment was intense, because I felt like everything was riding on this one phone call. I knew we wouldn't get any leads from anywhere else, so this had to be it.

"Good morning," Ari's mother sang into the phone in her everyday chipper voice.

"Morning. It's Skye," I sang back. I couldn't allow her to know that something was wrong, so I went into actress mode.

"Hey, lovely. Calling to check on your handsome man? He's so precious, Skye," she said with a smile plastered on her face that I could hear radiating through the phone.

He's there? Was I that lucky?

"Yes. What is my boy doing?" I said, playing along. I needed more information.

"He just finished devouring a bottle," she said with a chuckle.

I knew it was true. Cairo was his father's child. The boy could eat.

"Where is Ariana?" I asked, going out on a limb.

"Honestly, I have no idea. She and Cairo came over yesterday, and she was supposed to be heading out for a few hours. She hasn't called or anything," she explained.

"Well, I just got back into the city. Can I come pick up my boy? I miss him terribly," I said, sounding sad. That wasn't an act. I really did miss my boy, and the sooner I got him back, the better I would feel.

"Of course. I'm just glad I finally got to see him. I'll start getting his things ready now," she said.

"Okay. I'm on my way," I said, quickly hanging up the phone.

I didn't have time to waste. I needed to get Cairo before Ariana decided to call her mother or go back to her house. I got up off the bed and headed out of the room. Ty and Victoria were sitting in the living room in silence, but I didn't have time to deal with them either.

"I'll be back," I shouted over my shoulder as I headed out the front door to catch a taxi.

When the cab came to a complete stop in front of Ariana's mother's brownstone, I handed him a $50 bill and told him to keep the meter running. I needed to be in and out, so I hoped to God that she had Cairo ready like she said she would.

I stepped out of the cab and proceeded up the steps, two at a time, that led to her front door. I pushed the doorbell and shifted my weight to one side as I grew impatient. I hadn't even given her a minute to get to the door. I just didn't have a minute to waste.

When Ariana's mom finally opened the door holding Cairo, I felt a weight lift off my shoulders. I reached for my baby and thanked God.

"Cairo!" I squealed as I planted kisses all over his face.

"It was such a pleasure having him over. Let me get his bag," she said as she turned to head into the house.

"It's okay. Keep it for when he comes back to visit you. We gotta head out. His aunt wants to see him," I said as I backpedaled down the steps.

I promised to call her and told her that Cairo would be back soon, although that was the furthest thing from the truth. Once I was back within the safety of the taxi, I let out a hard breath and started to search my baby for bruises. There weren't any, and he appeared to be fine. He was smiling that soft, welcoming smile that made my heart flutter. I just knew he was as happy to see me as I was to see him.

"I love you so much, Cairo." I professed my love for him as if he could tell me he loved me back. I didn't need to hear it, though. I knew he did.

I was glad I opted to take a taxi. It gave me time to bask in the joy of having my baby boy back. I held him close to my heart with a grip that said I never wanted to let him go. I smothered him with kisses for the entire ride, and before I knew it, the taxi was pulling up in front of my building. I handed the driver another $50 bill before hitting the pavement and heading up to my place.

Chapter Three

Ty

I was in the kitchen looking for something to eat when I heard what sounded like a baby cooing. I missed Cai like crazy, but I knew a nigga wasn't going crazy and starting to hear shit. I looked over at Vic and saw her looking at me. We must have been thinking the same thing. Just when I was ready to go investigate the noise, Skye came prancing into the kitchen with Cairo in her arms. He was smiling and speaking the language that only he knew fluently, just as always. I never felt so good in my life.

"How? I mean, where?" I really couldn't get the questions out properly, but Skye understood.

She explained that something made her want to call Ariana's mother, and she did. One thing led to another, and here she was with Cairo safe. I guessed that mother's intuition shit was real. I could see a little bit of the old Skye resurface, but I knew she wouldn't be completely back until Ariana was handled.

"Ty," Skye spoke while taking a seat at the table.

"Yeah, wassup?" I questioned. I didn't have a clue what she wanted, but whatever it was, I was going to do it.

"I need you and Cairo on a plane back to Miami. I would have Victoria take him, but I know for a fact she is not going to want to leave. I just need Cairo somewhere safe. My mother is there, his grandmother, Hector, and his father. I know they won't let anything happen to him." Her tone told me she was dead serious, but I secretly hoped that she would change her mind.

What would happen if I left them here alone to go after Ari? I learned a while ago that niggas shouldn't really underestimate Skye. If she knew she could get to the bottom of this on her own, I had to respect it. Her track record didn't give me any reason not to.

"A'ight, sis. I'll take him. What do I tell Cam?" I asked, knowing that I needed to prepare to deal with the 101 questions my nigga would definitely ask.

"Nothing. Tell him I gave you Cairo and sent you back. It's not the complete story, but it's not a lie, either. I'll deal with Cameron when I get back to Miami, which hopefully will be tonight or tomorrow. Either way, I want Cairo where I know he can't be touched," she said, getting up and excusing herself from the table.

That gave me time to talk to Vic. I knew that having Cairo back would soften her a little bit, and hopefully she, too, would forgive me. I wanted shit between us to work, and whatever I needed to do to let her see that, I was willing to do.

"Vic," I said, trying to gain her attention. Instead, she rose from the table and walked out of the kitchen.

I was disappointed but definitely wasn't giving up yet. I ended up making a quick turkey sandwich. Just as I was taking the last bite, Skye walked into the kitchen and handed me Cairo.

"I'll text you the details. Your flight leaves in an hour and a half. Victoria is going to take y'all to the airport. Do not call anyone. I mean, nobody. As soon as your flight lands in Miami, call me, and once you reach the house, call me again," she said, kissing Cairo as Vic popped her head in the kitchen and signaled for me to come.

I hugged Skye and went out behind Vic.

Victoria

I honestly didn't want to take Ty and Cairo to the airport. Not because I was mad at Ty, but because I was in love with him and just didn't want to forgive him for fucking up so easily. Skye knew what she was doing, making me take them. He could have easily taken a taxi.

"Vic," Ty called out to me as I stopped at a red light.

I glanced to the back seat where he and Cairo were, and I gave him a half smile.

"I'm sorry," he said.

I knew he was. Ty would never do anything to intentionally put my nephew in harm's way. In fact, he wouldn't put any of us in harm's way, not just Cairo. I was still mad, though. I got that he felt some type of way because Ariana lost their baby, but shit, if my nephew had become collateral damage, there would have been hell to pay. I knew that I should let it go because Cairo was safe and back with us. I would, just not at that point in time.

Conversation was at a minimum. For the rest of the ride to JFK, the only sounds heard were the tunes that were playing through the radio at a very low volume. I didn't want to wake a sleeping Cairo. When we pulled up to the airport, I got out to kiss my nephew before they headed inside.

"Titi loves you, Cai," I said after I planted a kiss on his hand. I looked up at Ty. "Have a safe flight," I said and turned to get back in the car. I felt a strong hand grab my arm and force me to turn around, and that's when our lips met. My brain was screaming for me to back up and continue to play angry, but my tongue was dancing to a whole different tune. When we finally did break away from each other, I reached up and touched my lip.

Ty smiled and coolly said, "I love you, Vic," before turning and heading through the airport door.

I was left there stumped for a minute. He said he loved me. I knew he loved me like family all those years, but did that declaration of love mean, "I love you as my woman"? I knew it did, and that forced a smile on my face and a flutter in my heart.

I jumped back into Skye's whip and headed back to her house with completely happy thoughts. My nephew was safe, and Ty had told me he loved me for the first time. Nothing could bring me off that happy cloud. I was going to fully enjoy it even if it was only for the moment. I turned up the volume as Rihanna's song "Stay" came on, and I hit the highway.

When I got back to Skye's house, I found her sitting in the living room, scrolling through her phone like a madwoman. I never saw someone swipe the screen of their iPhone so fast and with so much force, ever. I flopped down beside her and let her know that they were safely at the airport and should be on their way to Miami. She nodded and thanked me without taking her eyes off the screen.

I just left her alone. I sat back and thought about how things would be once all this shit was over. I would have my man and my family. Skye had her man and her son. Things would be good. I just wished it would happen sooner rather than later.

The ringing of Skye's cell phone shook us both. The entire house was silent, so the random ringing startled us both. I looked over at her while she took a few breaths before sliding her finger across the screen to answer. I sat up and prepared to listen to her side of the conversation.

"Wassup?" Skye said to the caller on the other end of the line. There was a moment of silence before she started to speak again. "No, he don't mess with her anymore. Why you ask?"

I watched her demeanor change as she sat upright and became even more engrossed in the conversation than she was initially.

She popped up from her seat on the couch. "What!" she yelled into the phone.

By this time, she was pacing back and forth as she listened to the caller on the other end. Whatever was said had shaken Skye to the core. She was irate. When she hung up the phone, she snatched her car keys that I'd set down on the coffee table.

"Who was that on the phone?" I asked, getting up and stepping closer to her.

"It was James. I'll be back. Stay put and listen for my call," she said before running out the front door.

Something felt terribly off, and I knew calling Skye and begging for answers would get me nowhere.

Chapter Four

Ariana

"Fuck, baby, I'm about to cum!" I squealed as I tightened my grip on his head. My body began to convulse as it released my fluids all over his tongue.

He wasn't fazed. Like the pro he was, he licked and sucked every ounce of it until he was satisfied that he had cleaned up the mess he had helped create. I was on a cloud. This nigga's sex drive was always on one hundred. He had just finished digging my back out upstairs in the bedroom, and here he was eating the shit out of my pussy. Who was I to complain?

I looked down at him as he looked at me with a sexy-ass smirk on his face.

"I be back, shorty. I'm going to the bathroom," he said as he got up and headed to the bathroom.

I wanted to move, but I was spent. After the multiple orgasms I'd reached during our sex session to the amazing orgasm I'd just had from the best head ever, I couldn't move if my life depended on it. So I didn't bother.

I lay back and caught my breath as I thought about what was next. I needed to get back to my mother's before she started calling me off the hook, asking when I was going to pick up Cairo, but I figured a few more hours with my boo wouldn't hurt. Plus I wanted to talk to him about me having Cairo. I didn't want him to find out any other way, because I was really starting to fall for him.

The sound of his footsteps approaching let me know that he was done in the bathroom. I assumed he was cleaning my pussy juice off his face. I chuckled at the thought just as he sat down beside me on the couch and threw his arm over my shoulder.

"You good, baby?" He looked at me, chuckling.

"I am," I said in between planting a kiss on his cheek and then on his lips.

He grabbed the controller to his Xbox and started up a game of *2K*. I curled under his arm and watched him. I was waiting for the right moment to spring on the information on him. I hoped he wouldn't leave me. I was getting tired of letting niggas in my life only for them to walk right back out. It was time I got what I deserved and got my life back on track. Once I gave Cairo back and got the money, my baby and I could move anywhere we wanted and live comfortably. Hopefully start our own family.

Once he was done with his game of *2K,* I knew it was time to talk. Although I dreaded it, it needed to be done.

"Babe," I said in a whisper.

"Yeah, shorty, wassup?" he said, pulling me closer to him.

I took a deep breath and laid it all on the table, not leaving out one bit of information. If we had any chance of moving forward, I had to be honest.

"Fuck you mean, you kidnapped their baby?" he barked, pushing me away from him.

"You don't understand, babe," I started to explain.

"What the fuck is there to understand? I could give two fucks about Skye or Cam, but the baby ain't have shit to do with nothing. You took shit to a different level," he barked with his vein bulging out his forehead. I didn't anticipate him being that pissed off.

"Calm down. I'm not going to hurt him. Once Ty get up the two million dollars, I plan on giving him back," I said with pleading eyes.

The mention of the money calmed him down, and his whole demeanor changed.

"Two million dollars?" he asked.

"Yes. Do you know what we could do with that?"

Skye

I knew James had no idea what was going on between Ariana and me, so I knew he didn't think he was doing much damage by telling me the information he had. What started out as a phone call just to find out if Ty and Ariana were still together led me to that nigga's house. I thought back to everything James said. I wanted to make sure my next moves were calculated. Everything I did from that moment forward could have dire consequences.

"Yo, Ariana and Ty still together?" he'd asked as soon as I spoke into the phone.

"No, he don't mess with her anymore. Why you ask?" I was interested in knowing where the conversation was headed.

"I went to the nigga JR house to pick up some bread, and he was bragging about some chick he had just finished smashing. We laughed about it and shit, and then Ari came skipping into the living room. Look like she shit herself when she saw me. I didn't get into it. I just snatched up the money and bounced," he said, running down what happened when he went to JR's house.

Why JR? I checked my nine and made sure the silencer was screwed on before stepping out of the car and heading up the street where his house was located.

I stood outside his front door, still unable to process that Ariana was behind the kidnapping of Cairo. It seemed as if from the moment I decided to be with Cameron wholeheartedly, my friendship with Ariana was doomed. My heart was heavy because I never in a million years would have thought she would hurt me to this magnitude. I guessed she could say the same thing since I was the one who made the call to end her life. It was a necessary reaction to things she had done.

I couldn't take it any longer. The more I heard her speak freely about taking my son, the more my finger itched to squeeze the trigger of my nine until the clip emptied. Then there was him. I never thought he had balls. In my eyes, he was a soldier who did what he was told, and that would always be his position. I never saw him moving up in rank, but there he was in the flesh, not only showing that he had balls, but letting me know they were big. Everyone had an agenda. I kicked myself for it taking me so long to figure it all out. Since I took over Cam's business, I'd treated him like a brother. To cross Cameron was one thing, but me? He made more with me than what Cameron would have ever allowed him to make. It wasn't true what they said about money. I was slowing learning that pussy was truly the root of all evil.

I grew tired of watching them through the window and listening to them make plans with the money they thought they would gain by requesting a ransom. I'd heard enough, and at that point, I didn't care if I was outnumbered. This was something that needed to be handled, and regardless of the outcome, I was dead set on handling it.

Just as I made up my mind to force my way into the house, I saw him making his way toward the front door. I quickly ducked down behind the untrimmed bushes. I pressed my back flat against the house and held my breath until I heard the front door slam. I watched as he jogged down the driveway and hopped in his car.

I silently cursed because I was hoping to kill two birds with one stone. Surely it would happen another day. I didn't remember hearing the door lock after he stormed off, so I used that to my advantage. I stood from behind the bush, slipped on the leather gloves that were tucked in my back pocket, and slowly turned the doorknob. Just as I expected, the door was unlocked.

Dumb bitch. I tightened the grip on my nine and tiptoed toward the voice I heard having a one-sided conversation. I assumed Ariana was on the phone.

I found Ariana sitting in the living room, screaming through the phone at someone. She must have been having a bad day, but she wasn't aware of how much worse it was about to get. I crept up behind her and pressed the cold steel to her temple, snatching her cell phone out of her hand in the same motion. After ending the call, I contemplated speaking, but I wanted her to see who I was. I wanted Ariana to know I was her personal grim reaper. I wanted to make it clear that she'd crossed the wrong person.

I walked around the couch, bringing myself face-to-face with the girl I would have given my life for a year ago. The look on her face was priceless, but still, she gave me a smug look as if she had no worries.

"Kill me and you will never find Cairo," Ariana said, staring down at the barrel of my gun.

I let out a hearty laugh, one of those types of laughs where you grab your stomach and lean over like you have stomach cramps because it was so funny.

"You really thought that we would never find Cairo? You left him with the most obvious person, you stupid bitch," I barked, taking a step closer to her.

I watched the look of defeat come over her as I placed my gun on the end table. I reached forward and pulled Ariana to her feet by the skimpy puff she called a ponytail. I guessed she was so pressed for money that she wasn't rocking her normal weave.

I took a step back and threw up my hands. Although I knew how this would end, I wanted to give Ariana a chance to have a one-on-one with me. It was what she always secretly wanted. Her throwing her hands up signaled to me that she had indeed accepted my challenge. I leaned forward and threw a left hook that connected with her jaw, causing her to stumble back. She didn't fall, but I used the seconds when she tried to compose herself to land blow after blow to her midsection.

I screamed obscenities as I continued to deliver haymakers and hooks, each blow hitting the intended target body part. I managed to get Ariana in a headlock, and then I raised my leg and pushed her head down simultaneously, crashing my knee into her nose. Hearing her cry out in pain only made me want to go harder. I wanted her silenced for good, and I was completely prepared to do it with my bare hands. I had the upper hand until I tripped over the coffee table. I fell backward onto the floor, bringing Ariana down with me.

If I hadn't already knocked the wind out of her, she probably would have gotten the best of me since she was now on top. Her blows weren't fazing me. She was weak, and she knew it. I trailed her line of sight. When her eyes landed on my gun, I knew I had to get to it first. Between receiving and reciprocating punches, we tussled and knocked over the end table. I crawled toward the gun, and Ariana caught my leg. I tried to kick her to break free and continue my pursuit for the gun, but it was to no avail. The tussle continued. Ariana delivered a blow to the side of my head that damn near crippled me. In that split second, she was able to get her hands on the gun. Giving up wasn't an option, so I channeled all the energy I could and lunged toward her. We ended up in an intense struggle, me to gain possession of the gun and her to let off the shot that would instantly end my life.

It all started to happen at an extremely fast past. Just as the gun went off, I saw a shadowy figure move in the corner of my eye.

"Nooo," Victoria screamed.

I hadn't a clue how she had got there. I wished she had made it sooner. Thoughts of Cairo flashed through my mind as I felt the blood seeping through my shirt. It only took me a second to realize I wasn't the one who got shot. I hadn't pulled the trigger, either. I pushed Ariana's stiff body off of me and found Victoria frozen with the gun still in her hand.

Evidently, she was in shock. She had just committed her first murder. I pulled myself up off the floor and walked over to her. Gripping the butt of the gun, I slowly tugged it out of her grasp.

"I thought she was . . . I don't know. I panicked. I couldn't let anything happen to you, sis, which is why I called James. Once he told me what he told you, I knew I needed to get to you," she tried to explain.

I looked back at Ariana's dead body and hung my head low. I didn't know what to say to Victoria. One thing was for sure, though. She had saved my life.

"You saved my life, Victoria. Thank you." I pulled her into me for an embrace.

"You would have done it for me," she said, finally gaining the ability to coherently speak.

"In a heartbeat. We gotta go. I'm sure someone heard your gun go off and called the cops," I stated as I walked over to where Ariana's body lay and picked up my gun.

I kneeled down beside her and checked for a pulse. When I was sure there wasn't one, I returned to Victoria's side.

"Did you touch anything?" I asked, wondering if she had left prints.

"No. I mean, the door. That's it," she said as contemplation settled in her expression.

I could hear the sirens and knew we were running out of time. We both definitely wouldn't make it out undetected. I knew what needed to be done. I just hoped like hell my plan would work.

"Victoria, take these guns. Go through the back. Do not touch anything with your bare hands. Walk a few blocks away and catch a taxi. Call JR and have him meet you at one of the spots. Don't mention anything that happened here. I don't know how you will do it, but get his prints on your gun. Wipe yours off first! Here, take these gloves."

I quickly removed my gloves and handed them to her.

"Once you got his prints on your gun, take the gun and stash it somewhere else. Don't tell anyone where it is. Please follow my instructions," I pleaded with her.

"I'm not leaving you here to take the fall. I did it, not you," Victoria said on the brink of crying.

"Victoria, do you not hear the sirens? Get the fuck outta here. Now! I will call you!" I walked toward her and shoved her in the direction of the back door.

After a moment of hesitation, she left. I pulled out my cell phone and dialed 911 as I headed to the front door. After wiping Victoria's prints off the front doorknob with my shirt, I sat on the porch and told the police operator my version of what happened. I sat on the porch and went into actress mode. I needed to appear shaken. I needed tears. The only thing that made me sad was the thought of not seeing my son again if my plan didn't work. I thought about Cairo's precious face and how I longed to hold him in my arms, and the tears flowed freely.

As four police cars came to a stop in front of the house, I watched as uniformed officers jumped out with their guns drawn. Before doing anything else, I put my hands in the air. I wasn't trying to give those cops a reason to open fire. I sat with my hands in the air until I was approached by two female officers. They snatched me to my feet and threw cuffs on me while the other officers entered the house.

"Why am I in cuffs?" I questioned although I knew I wasn't saying anything until I got to the station.

I heard the officers shout some type of code, which I assumed was signaling them that there was a body.

"You want to tell us what happened that resulted in a dead body?" the tall, dark-skinned policewoman asked. She reminded me of Lisa Leslie. She didn't have a cop look at all, which made it hard for me to take her seriously.

"Not really," I answered nonchalantly. In order for this plan to work, I couldn't speak to anyone except my mother.

"Have it your way. We'll get the answers we need at the station," the other policewoman stated as she grabbed me and walked me toward the police cruiser. Her partner read me my rights.

Once they tossed me in the back seat, the tall one spoke through her walkie-talkie, and we were on our way.

Chapter Five

Victoria

"Fuck!" I cursed out loud as I walked down the street to where I'd had the cab drop me off when I came.

I looked down at my hands, and they were trembling. It wasn't because I had killed Ariana. Her life meant nothing to me once she decided to fuck with my family. Skye, on the other hand, had me worried. I couldn't believe I'd left her there. I prayed that whatever she had planned would work in our favor as I pulled out my phone and searched for JR's name in my contacts. I remembered I needed a taxi, so I called first before finding JR's name once again. I hit call and listened as the phone rang four times before he decided to answer.

"What up, Vic?" He spoke as if he didn't have a care in the world.

"Hey, JR. What you doing?" I asked, hoping he was free and close by.

"Shit. I'm in the east by Tae crib and shit. Just chillin'. What up, though? You need me?" He sounded like he was a real nigga. Too bad he was a snake.

"Yeah, can you meet me at the east spot? I'll be there in like twenty," I said, hoping that he would come.

"Yeah, I got you," he said before we ended the conversation.

I contemplated calling my brother, but there was really nothing he could possibly do. In addition to that, I needed to stick to Skye's plan. She had given me specific instructions, and I had to follow through. I clutched my purse close to me and waited a few more minutes for the cab to pull up. When it did, I slid into the back seat and got comfortable. As we headed toward East New York, I put on Skye's gloves and buried her gun at the bottom of my bag, leaving mine at the top.

When the cab pulled up to the spot, I repeated, *Skye's life depends on it,* over and over to myself before paying and stepping out of the car. I spotted JR's car and knew he was there already. I took a deep breath and headed inside. I definitely forgot to tell him to show up alone, but thankfully he did just that. As I got closer to him, I had no idea what I was going to say, but I knew I needed to come up with something and fast.

"What up, punk?" I said as I placed my bag on the table he was sitting at.

"Nothing. What up? What you doing out here?" he asked, eyeing me suspiciously.

"You know my nephew is missing, so I'm out here with my ear to the street, ready to body anything. That's kind of why I called you here," I said, reeling him in.

"Shit crazy. Who the fuck would go after Cai? Shit got me fucked up, but whatever I can do to help, I got you," he said. If the circumstances were any different, I would have believed him.

"I need another burner. The shit I got not going to get the job done." *Please take the bait.*

"What you got on you?" he inquired.

"It's in the bag." This was it, make it or break it.

He dug into my bag, biting the bait, and pulled out the murder weapon.

"What damage you thought you was going to do with a nine? Shit can do a little something, but you don't know who you up against," he said, inspecting the gun and leaving behind all the prints I needed.

"That's why I called you," I said, laughing. I was sure he thought I was laughing at his comment, but I was actually laughing at how fucking stupid he was.

"A'ight, I got you. Let me make some calls, and once I get something, I'll hit you up," he said as he put the gun back into my bag.

"Thanks, JR. You a lifesaver. I'm about to get up out of here, though. I'm hungry as I don't know what. Don't forget to call me," I said, turning to head to the door.

He got up and walked behind me. "Yeah. I'ma head back to Tae crib and whoop that nigga in some *2K*, but I got you. I won't forget," he said, climbing into his car.

Cabs ran frequently through this neighborhood, so there was no need for me to call one. I stood on the corner, and a minute later, I was in a cab and heading back to Skye's place to wait for her call, a call I prayed would come with good news.

Skye

The room they had me in was cold as I didn't know what. I was tempted to ask for a blanket. I was a mixture of annoyed and amused by the two cops who were trying to play "good cop/bad cop." The female detective was trying her hardest to sweet-talk me into a confession while her male counterpart was rough. He cursed me out and threatened me with a life sentence. I wouldn't budge. They had no idea who they were dealing with. I was a law student. Granted, I'd only completed a semester, but I knew my shit.

I sat there and stared off into space while they continued to "almost make me crack." That's what they kept saying every time their captain came in to check on their progress. I was growing tired of the antics. The back-and-

forth thing was getting old. It was time for me to speed
the process along.

"I want my lawyer," I said, grabbing the pen and pad
they had in front of me that was supposed to be used
for me to write a confession. Instead, I wrote down my
mother's name and number and slid it back to the officers.

"Once we call your lawyer, we are taking all deals off
the table," the male officer uttered.

"Call her," I said and put my head down on the table.

My mother was in Miami, so I knew I would be in here
for a minute. I was exhausted, but there was no way I
would be sleeping until I was home. Forty-five minutes
later, the female detective came back into the interrogation room to escort me to the holding cell.

"I'm owed a phone call, aren't I?" I said with sarcasm.

She sucked her teeth and led me to the phone, where
I was allowed to make one call. Since I knew they were
contacting my mother, I decided to call Victoria.

"Hello," she answered on the first ring.

"Hey, sis. Everything good?" I asked in reference to her
handling what she needed to handle with JR.

"Yes. What's going on with you?" she questioned.

I was relieved that she'd handled what I needed her
to do. "I'm all right. I will probably be in lockup for
the night. Depends how fast my mother can get down
here. Don't worry about me, though. I'm good," I stated,
trying to reassure her that I would be fine. That's when I
remembered I wouldn't be able to get any calls. "Did you
speak to Ty? Did he and Cairo get to Miami safely?"

"Yes, they touched down right before you called me. He
said he got the voicemail on your end, so he hit me up. I
didn't tell him what's going on, though," she explained.

The detective was signaling for me to wrap it up.
"A'ight, good. I gotta go. Go back to Miami now," I said
before ending the call.

The detective returned and escorted me to the holding cell that would be home to me for the next few hours. The cell was colder than the room and much more uncomfortable. I would have rather been in interrogation getting screamed at by the detectives versus sitting in this small-ass cell with three other females who all looked as if they were prostitutes. My eyes were heavy, and I felt myself battling to stay awake. I refused to sleep. The flight from here to Miami was only a few hours, so I was expecting my mother very soon.

Chapter Six

Cameron

I thought I was dreaming, hearing Cairo's cries, but as the cries got closer, I forced my eyes open. Seeing my nigga Ty walking into the family room with my son in his arms brought a feeling over me I hadn't felt in a while. I pulled myself up from lying across the couch and reached my arms out for my prince.

"Where's Skye? Where was he?" I demanded. I needed answers, and I needed them right then.

"She and Vic still in New York, bro. I really don't have the answers you need. Skye hit me and told me to come get him and bring him to you. That's what I did," Ty responded as he walked back out of the living room.

I knew he wasn't telling me the entire story, but I wasn't going to stress it. My little man was home, and I was sure Skye would be back soon too, so I was content for the moment. I was definitely going to get all the answers I wanted, but at the time, I just wanted to enjoy having my li'l man back.

"Cai, Daddy missed you, boy," I spoke to him as if he were a big boy. It didn't matter that he didn't understand. I made it my business to let my son know how much I loved him. That was one thing he would never have to doubt in his life. If I didn't make it to see tomorrow, he would know that I loved him.

It wasn't even a whole five minutes before my moms and Skye's moms came into the living room to see Cairo. They asked the same questions I did, but I didn't have any answers for them. That angered them, but they suppressed the anger and just accepted the fact that whatever happened, happened, and Cairo was home safe.

Adriana was in the middle of rocking Cairo as he dozed off when her phone started ringing. She handed him to me and accepted the call. Her entire demeanor changed, and the look on her face told me that it was about Skye. I felt like I was going to throw up, assuming the worst. It was like once one thing got back on track, another thing derailed. We'd just gotten Cai back, and now some shit had popped off with Skye. When was it going to end?

My mother and I waited patiently for Adriana to get off the phone, and when she did, she hit us with some left-field shit, something I never expected to happen.

"Skye has been arrested," she said as she stood up from her seat on the couch.

"For what?" I inquired. What could she have done so bad that it landed her in jail?

"Murder," she flatly stated before walking off.

My mother went behind her, but I couldn't move quickly even if I wanted to. I was stuck. Cairo was sleeping in my arms, and I was lost. My girl, my son's mother, was facing a murder wrap. Shit really couldn't get any worse. Skye may have had heart, but she wasn't built for jail. She definitely wasn't built to face a murder charge.

My mother returned to my and Cairo's side in the living room ten minutes after following Adriana out. She let me know Adriana had left and would call us as soon as she had more details. That wasn't satisfying enough. I couldn't stomach my girl sitting in a jail cell. It was a much better outcome than what I'd thought the phone call was about, but it wasn't good in the least.

I wondered if Ty knew about this shit. If he did and was keeping it from me, it was time for me to dead that nigga. The secret shit needed to be over. It was causing more problems than solving them.

My moms took Cairo from me and headed upstairs. I texted Ty and told him to come meet me in the living room. It was time we kicked it like we did back in the day. I'd never had to worry about Ty keeping shit from me, and the fact that I felt like that now didn't sit well with me at all.

My phone vibrated, alerting me that I had a new notification. I looked down and saw Ty's name on the screen. After punching in my code, I went to check the message.

Bro, I'm dead-ass tired. We'll kick it in the a.m.

What type of shit was he on? Now he was avoiding me?

Skye

Nearly four hours later, my name was being called. I was sitting straight up on the bench with my eyes glued to the bars, hoping and praying that my mother would show up. So to hear my name finally being called was like music to my ears.

This was a totally different detective from the one who brought me to holding earlier. I guessed the shifts had changed. She was much nicer. She didn't grab on me like I was nothing. She held on to my arm just to lead the way. I was led back to the interrogation room, where my mother was sitting with another detective. The look on her face caused me to drop my head and stare at the Maison Margiela sneakers that adorned my feet. I couldn't bear to see the look of disappointment in her face.

I sat down in the seat beside her and didn't say a word. She cleared her throat and began to give the detectives a tongue ass whooping that only she knew how to serve. My mother really was the best at what she did for a living.

"What are the charges?" she asked in a very nonchalant manner.

"Murder one. Unless she cooperates," the husky male detective said.

My mother looked at me then back to the detective before cracking a smile. "Let's go, Skye. Officer, when you have some chargers that could stick, she'll be around," she said before she headed to the door. I didn't hesitate to follow her.

I knew that they couldn't hold me there. They had absolutely no proof that I committed a crime. They were banking on me talking myself into a ditch, but I knew much better than that. All I had to do was wait it out until my mother came, like I did, and I was straight.

I wanted to head straight to Miami, but my mother said it would be best if I stuck around in case I had to go back to the station. I didn't mind sticking around New York a few extra days while they tried their hardest to solve a crime that only Victoria and I had the solution to. Although I wanted to see my baby, I knew he was okay, so a few more days away were okay with me.

On the cab ride to my parents' house, my mother didn't say one word. She shook her leg up and down, and I knew exactly what that meant. She was fuming, and I understood why. Why wouldn't she be? Her daughter was the suspect in a murder case. Although I would never have to stand up in court, the thought still pissed me off, so she was pissed off.

When we got in the house, my mother wasted no time before ripping me a new one. "Murder, Skye?" she screamed. "This shit has gone too fucking far. My child? Facing a murder charge. What the fuck has gotten into you?" She drove her fingers into my chest as she continued to scream.

"Mom, I swear to you I didn't kill Ariana. I was there, I know who did it, but it wasn't me," I pleaded, hoping she would hear me out.

"What the fuck were you even doing there, Skye? You do realize how this shit looks?" she questioned, lowering her voice. She knew that I wouldn't lie to her, so by me telling her that I didn't commit murder calmed her down a bit, but she was still upset because I was still facing the charge.

"Mom, I know how it looks, but it won't go any further than this." I took a seat on the couch and told her everything that had happened, from me ordering to have Ariana killed to how I ended up at JR's house. I even told her that it was indeed Victoria who pulled the trigger. My mother would never throw Victoria to the wolves, because she was family. She was my son's aunt, and my mother would protect her just as she was going to protect me.

"This is so much to take in. What is your plan? Where is the murder weapon?" she asked.

That was a good question, because I had no idea where it was. I just prayed Victoria hadn't left it at my house. If I knew the justice system like I thought I did, they were definitely going to show up at my place tomorrow with a warrant.

"I don't know. Victoria did what she needed to do and got JR's prints on the gun. I told her once she did that to stash it. I don't know how involved JR was with the kidnapping of Cairo, but I'm going to leave that to Ty and Cameron to figure out. Like you said, it has gone too far, and I told God that if He got me Cairo back, I would change. I want to. The gun is just an insurance policy. They won't find proof to send me or JR to trial, but if it came down to me or him, that gun will surface," I explained and hoped that she understood.

"It's been a very long night. Let's get some sleep, and we'll pick this back up in the morning," she said, standing to leave.

"Where is Dad?" I called out after her.

"He is overseas doing some scouting. He'll be gone for another three or four weeks. We'll keep this from him until he is home. We don't want him stressed out while he is away working. Understand?" she said.

I nodded, and she walked off. I wasn't far behind. I headed upstairs for a hot shower, then climbed into my bed. Sleep wasn't far behind. I was beyond beat.

Cameron

I glanced at the time on the alarm clock and sucked my teeth. It read 6:45 a.m., which brought the number of hours I'd lain in bed, tossing and turning to seven. I hadn't been able to sleep because I was worried about Skye. She was putting up a tough exterior, but she was in no way, shape, or form built for jail. I knew that for sure. I sat up in bed and reached for my cane.

"Dumb-ass shit!" I spoke in frustration.

I was over having to get around with my third leg. The cotton-like feeling in my mouth made me suppress my frustrations as I needed the cane to go get a bot-tle of water. After a minute of getting myself together,

I was up with the assistance of my cane and heading to the kitchen. I walked in looking to grab a bottle of water and head back to bed, but I found Ty sitting at the counter with a big-ass bowl of Cap'n Crunch.

"What up?" I said, opening the refrigerator and getting the water.

"Couldn't sleep," Ty said, taking a spoonful of his cereal.

There was commotion coming from the foyer that grabbed our attention. Ty got up and started to walk ahead of me as if he needed to assess the situation like I was a little nigga or something. I grabbed my cane and made my way to his side. We walked up on Hector coming in with three other Spanish cats. Two were built like guards, so I assumed they were, especially by the way they stood directly behind the old Spanish dude. He had to be Skye's grandfather. I'd heard about ol' dude before I even knew Skye was his granddaughter. I'd just never met him in person before.

"Wassup, Hector," I spoke, alerting them that we were in their presence.

"Wassup, Cameron. This is Skye's grandfather," Hector said, confirming my assumption.

"Nice to meet you, Andreas," I said, reaching my hand out to shake his.

"Did we grow up together?" he asked, swatting my hand away.

Nigga lucky he's Skye's grandfather. I was tempted to steal on his old ass. Who the fuck this dude thought he was, Bugsy Siegel? I really couldn't imagine him putting in the work or having the amount of clout he did. He was a pretty-looking nigga. He even rocked curly hair like he was related to El and Chico DeBarge. He had much more hang time, though. Feeling my legs quiver due to me standing for too long, I knew it was time to sit down. I said my goodbyes and started toward the living room.

"Actually, Cameron, I think we should talk," the unknown DeBarge brother spoke, stopping me in my tracks.

I pointed toward the living room and hoped he got the message. I wasn't even on no funny shit. I really did just need to sit down. Once I was seated, Ty came strolling in behind me like I knew he would. We didn't know them niggas from Adam. Related to Skye or not, they were still strangers in my book. Moments after Ty and I were settled in the living room, Andreas came in. I thought he would have come alone, but his two John Cena looking-ass guards came with him.

He sat in the chair that was closest to the fireplace and drank from the bottle of water Hector handed him. Andreas sat in silence for a minute as he looked over at Ty then back to me.

"Cameron, my question for you is, how did you let this happen?" Andreas asked, readjusting his position in his seat.

I was confused. Did he not know all that was going on? How the fuck was I supposed to protect Skye from getting locked up? She didn't even tell me what was going on before she dipped. "No disrespect, sir—" I began to speak but was cut short.

"'No disrespect' is what a person says right before they disrespect you. Try again. Or was it your intention to disrespect me?" Andreas asked, never taking his eyes off me.

If I didn't have love for Skye, I would have definitely said fuck that old nigga and gone back to my room. It was early as shit, and quite frankly, I didn't want, nor did I need to listen to his shit.

"Nah, it wasn't my intention to disrespect you. I really don't know how to answer your question, though. I'm in no position to chase Skye around state to state. She keeps me in the dark, so how much could I possibly do for her?"

I spoke, feeling confident in my answer.

"If you think there was nothing for you to do, you have a lot to learn. Maybe you aren't fit to be in this business. It is your duty to protect your family, Cameron, even if you had to do it from your grave. You should always have things in motion to ensure your family is good. Skye should have never known what the inside of a jail cell looked like. You have men there in NYC. Why is it none of them have tabs on her? Is this how y'all operate? If Skye decides to step down, which I will be recommending to her, how am I to trust you with my product if I can't trust you with my granddaughter?" Andreas spoke before taking another sip of his water.

I couldn't answer him right away, because in a sense he was right. I should have been, at any given moment, able to call one of my niggas and ask if they had the drop on Skye. I couldn't, though. Andreas must have sensed that I didn't have an answer for him, because he continued to talk.

At first, I thought everything he was saying wasn't beneficial to me or how I ran my shit, but he started to really make sense. He schooled me and Ty on shit we would have never thought about previously. Andreas was starting to sound like the Poppy I heard stories about. He was indeed that nigga. I didn't know if it was a good or bad thing having him here in Miami with us. Rumor had it he only left Panama if it was an emergency, and whoever called for that would be sure to suffer dire consequences. Even with having him sitting in my living room, I couldn't believe he was actually Skye's grandfather. No wonder it was so easy for her to take over my shit. It was in her blood.

I remembered the first time I ever heard about him. It wasn't a pleasant story at all. I had to have been about 9 or 10 years old. My pops was on the phone with Jeff, telling him about some Panamanian dude who was supplying the entire East Coast and a majority of the West. From what I gathered from the conversation, he had some type of VIP client list. Never would he just deal with a regular nigga looking for work. He dealt with bosses, and back then, he just didn't think my pops was on that level, so he declined his business. My father, being the nigga he was, took that as motivation to grind harder. He respected how Andreas ran his business. Shit, it made sense to me. If you wanted your shit to stay an A1 operation, you had to only associate with A1 niggas. It definitely explained why Poppy had been around as long as he had. He'd never served a day in prison, and as far as I knew, he didn't have niggas gunning for him, either. He had beef here and there, but he always shut it down, resulting in body parts of his enemies being delivered to their families.

That's the story my pops told Jeff when Jeff wanted to flip out because Andreas denied them. My pops told him about a local dealer named G. G was a young nigga who lived in Canarsie back then. He and his boys actually worked up the courage and tried to go toe-to-toe with Andreas after being denied also. G took a trip to Panama with his boys, ready to put in work. It was the last time he and his boys were heard or seen until their body parts started popping up randomly around the city. Andreas sent a message, and the message was heard loud and clear.

Throughout the years, I'd heard about other encounters that niggas had with Andreas, but they didn't get to live to tell their stories. I never thought I would encounter him, because my dad had Miguel's family as a connect since back in the day. Our business with the Mexicans was always on point, and we never came across any problems until now. I felt like meeting Skye was destiny, not just because I knew she was the one for me, but having Andreas on my team was exactly what niggas needed to go to the next level. I just had to show him that I was that guy. I definitely had to prove to him that the safety of my family came first.

Chapter Seven

Poppy

It was bad enough that I had to take an impromptu trip to the States after hearing my granddaughter was arrested. Now I had to deal with these two little shits who knew nothing. The new-school businessmen handled things way different from how we handled it in my day. However, I'd heard the stories, and I knew that, with a little molding, Cameron could really be a force in this business. I planned on guiding him where he needed to be, but first I needed to make sure his priorities were intact. He couldn't do much about what happened while he was in a coma, but at least now I had him thinking. In the event that something of this magnitude happened again, he'd be better prepared.

I didn't know what it was that I saw in Cameron. Maybe I saw my son in him. Everything about his relationship with Skye made me think about Andreas Jr. I made the same mistake Cameron made when I was just starting out in this business. I wasn't ready, though, nor was I molded for it. My father, Renaldo, was murdered when I was 15 years old. I remembered the day like it just happened. We had just returned from shopping to find several masked men in our home waiting for us. My mother, Amelia, was spread out on the couch with her eyes wide open. At first glance, I thought she was watching the scene unfold. Then I noticed the tiny bullet hole in the center of her forehead. It wasn't the first time I had seen a dead body, but because it was my mother, it hurt me deep.

There were words shared between my father and the guys before they gave him the same treatment they gave to my mother. I watched his lifeless body fall at my feet. His eyes were wide open as well, and I stared into them while the masked men searched my house in efforts to retrieve money and whatever else they could. 'Til present day I couldn't understand why they left me alive. I was just thankful they did. It gave me the chance to avenge my parents' deaths.

I had an uncle who was ready and willing to take over the business upon my father's demise, but he was shady, and I knew it. I would have rather seen the business fall to pieces than leave it in the hands of a sheist master. I did neither, and instead, I gathered all the information my father had locked away in various safes, and I took over myself. No one knew how unprepared I was because I didn't let it show, nor did I speak it. Shit was going well until I met my ex-wife, Jennifer, Adriana's mother.

That's when the one and only mistake I'd made to date came back to me in the worst way. Like Cameron, I thought I had shit under total control. Everyone respected me, and my men were loyal. I was young and wealthy, and I had the most beautiful woman in my bed every night. In my eyes, I was untouchable. Jennifer gave birth to AJ a year after we got together and Adriana one year after that, and life was perfect. I couldn't ask for anything more. I had my wife and beautiful children. It was true when they say all good things must come to an end, because they did.

When Jennifer decided to leave me, I got custody of AJ. I thought it was a good idea back then. However, now much older and way wiser, I saw that it wasn't. For many years, everything was okay with AJ living with me, until he was 16 years old and decided he wanted parts. I wasn't going to avoid the inevitable, so I allowed it. I felt respected enough and feared enough that no one would try my son.

During one of my many visits to the States to try to make things better with Jennifer in hopes that I could see Adriana, something went terribly wrong. I returned home to find that my son had been murdered in cold blood. Although I wanted to seek revenge for his death, I never had to. Someone had surprised me and stepped up to the plate. I felt good about that but still carried guilt for what had happened to him.

From that day on, I had a different view on life and how I ran my business. I changed my way of acting and never had the same problem since. If I could have, I would have helped Cameron see those things without him having to lose Skye or his son. It was my point for speaking to him in such a manner. He may not have understood it at that moment, but he would. I would make sure of that.

I schooled Cameron and Ty on a few more things before deciding they'd had enough. I had only been in Miami for a few hours and didn't want to spend the entire day talking. We had to get to the bottom of what was going on within their organization that had led to the kidnapping of Cairo and Skye landing in jail.

"I want to wash the travel off of me and get a few hours of sleep. We'll pick up where we left off a little later on. Oh, and Poppy or Pop Pop will suffice. My school comrades call me Andreas," I said, rising from the chair I'd occupied.

We said our goodbyes before Hector showed me to the room I would be staying in for the duration of my trip. Once I was settled in, George and Nelson were given instructions to head back to Panama. They were used to ensure my safe arrival. Now that I was settled in, they were no longer needed as long as Hector was around. I planned for this trip to be longer than my normal trip to the States as there was much more that needed to be done. First things first were a shower and a little bit of rest.

Skye

As I stepped out of Miami International, I sighed a bit of relief. We spent a few extra days in New York while the investigation was underway. They were coming up empty at every corner they turned even after questioning JR. I would have to face him soon since he was now aware that I was indeed at his house that day, but I wasn't worried about that. I was looking forward to it. I really did plan on keeping up my end of the deal I made with God. Cairo was home and safe, so it was indeed time for me to change my ways.

Although the investigation was ongoing, I pushed all thought about it to the back of my mind. There was no real reason for me to stress over it. I was in the clear. The detectives thought I was guilty, but what mattered was what they could prove, and that was nothing.

I took a few calls from Ariana's mother at first, but once she found out that I was a suspect, her calling just for a shoulder to cry on turned into empty threats. I didn't have time for that, either. Thoughts of her were pushed back into the corner of my memory bank with all other details of the incident. I was looking toward my future with my son and, hopefully, Cameron. It was time for me to get back to being me.

"Mom, who picking us up?" I asked as we headed down the street where numerous cars were loading and unloading passengers.

"Hector," she answered, not really wanting to acknowledge that I was in her presence. My mother was still very much pissed over the entire ordeal. I knew that she understood why I did what I did and the position I was in, but what mother wanted to defend her child in a murder trial? I respected her being angry, so I left her alone.

Once we reached Hector, I hugged him as he told me it was nice to have me back before I slid into the back seat of the car. The entire ride to the house I spent staring out the window thinking about the most important person in my world: Cairo.

I couldn't wait to see my baby and hold him. Shit, I was even looking forward to changing his shitty diapers. The joys of being a mother. That was the moment for me. I thanked God for keeping me alive and sane thus far as well as for bringing my son back. I apologized for all the wrong I'd done and asked for His forgiveness. In exchange, I vowed to be done. After everything settled down, I didn't want any more part of this life. At first, I was doing what I needed to do for Cameron and his family, but it was about Cairo now.

When we pulled up to the house, I didn't even allow the car to come to a complete stop before opening my door and getting out. I expeditiously approached the front door, ready to see my boy. I dug into my Chanel bag to retrieve my keys and let myself in. As I walked into the house, the aroma of good cooking hit me smack dead in the face.

I migrated to the kitchen to find Mariah cooking and Cameron and Cairo sitting at the counter, keeping her company.

"Hey," I said to get their attention.

"Skye, thank God. I'm so happy to have you home. Girl, what the hell is wrong with you?" Mariah said while remaining focused on the dish she was preparing.

"I don't really want to talk about it. Cairo!" I switched the subject, not wanting to indulge in that story. It happened, and I was moving forward.

I sat at the counter next to Cameron, who had yet to speak to me, and reached for my son. He passed him to me before grabbing his cane and rising to make his exit. I really couldn't have cared less at the moment.

"Hi, Mommy's boy," I cooed at Cairo and planted soft kisses on his cheeks.

His smile was so warm and inviting for a baby. He would have the exact same charm his father possessed.

"Your grandfather is here, Skye," Mariah said, giving me a heads-up.

I felt my heart sink to the bottom of my stomach. I was prepared to deal with everyone except him. "What you mean he is here? Like in Miami?" I asked, confused.

"Yep, he's been here since the day after your mother left to get you. Right now, he's out with Ty and Victoria. I don't know where they went," she explained.

Good thing he wasn't home yet. I had a bit more time to figure out exactly what I would say to him to keep him from going off on me.

Mariah was on a roll. She continued to speak even though I was trying to enjoy my time with my son. She disregarded that. "I don't know what's going on with you and Cameron, but y'all need to fix it."

"They really do," my mother said, walking into the kitchen and joining Cairo and me at the counter. She reached for Cairo and took him out of my arms. I didn't protest, although I really wanted to.

"We'll talk sooner or later," I said, not really wanting to have that conversation either.

"You're not busy. Go talk now. Fix whatever the issue is, because this shit is old and tired," my mother said in a "test me if you want to" voice.

I knew better to give a rebuttal. I was already on her bad side and didn't want to butt heads with her again. I kissed my son and headed to Cameron's room, where I knew he would be. The door was closed, but I didn't care. I walked right on in.

Cameron

Hearing someone walk into my room, I pressed pause on the controller and looked up from the game of *Black Ops* I was playing at the moment. My eyes met hers. Skye was still the most gorgeous female walking the earth to me. I just couldn't get past it. She'd risked her life and, even worse than that, the life of our child. For what? I just didn't think it was worth it. To make matters worse, I was here, and she still thought she needed to handle my business. She fucked around and landed herself in jail. What type of shit was she on?

"You really not going to speak to me?" she said as she walked farther into my room.

I watched her closely. The closer she got, the more I felt the urge to snatch her little ass up and fuck all the smart shit she was gonna say right out of her. My dick twitched at the thought of sliding in that. It'd been a minute.

"Cameron, really, what the fuck is your problem?" she spat.

So much for that.

"Real shit, Skye, watch your mouth. I know you been running around here the last few months like you was that nigga, but that ain't you, shorty." I spoke just above a whisper but sternly enough for her to understand that I wasn't in the business of playing games with her.

"What running around like I was that nigga? You got to be shitting me. I did everything I did for you. Any nigga would have been glad to have a chick like me willing to do anything for him. You an unappreciative bastard. You blaming me for what exactly? I'm here. Our son was born extremely healthy, and he's here. Cairo was kidnapped, and I got him back. Me, nigga! So what the fuck you up in here mad about? Because you can't run the street like you want? Because you still have therapy? Get the fuck over it. Niggas get shot every day. You here, and instead of acting like you having your fucking period, you should be thankful that you get to watch your son grow up. Soon you will be able to chase him up and down a basketball court. Or would you rather never have the ability to walk again? Get your shit together for real. I'm tired of this same routine with you. It's old. I don't even want a thank-you. I don't want you to acknowledge that I did what needed to be done. I just really want you to get it together."

I looked away from her and hit the button on the controller, starting the game back up. Before I knew it, the controller was snatched out my hand. I looked up at Skye like she was crazy as she threw the controller, sending it crashing into the wall.

"Don't disrespect me like that," she barked, coming closer to me.

I grabbed my cane and got up off the bed. I had to be prepared for whatever she planned on doing next.

"You getting up like you going to do something. Nigga, sit the fuck back down," she yelled, pointing her finger in my face.

Who was that girl? She definitely wasn't the female I thought I was going to spend the rest of my life with. When did shit even get this bad?

"You think because you spent a night or two in bookings you bad? I don't get how you could be so smart yet so fucking dumb at the same time. Who purposely gets themselves locked up for a crime they claim they didn't commit? That shit was stupid and reckless," I yelled back at her.

"You have no idea what you're talking about, that's the funny thing. You swear you know everything. In actuality, you don't know shit. In your words, I don't get how you could be so smart yet so fucking dumb at the same time. But you know what?"

Her demeanor changed as she spoke. The anger was gone. It was as if she were a different person. I wasn't in the mood for that multiple personality shit, so I cut her off.

"Nah, I don't know, and to keep it trill, I don't even care at this point," I said, laying my cane back against the nightstand and sitting back down on the bed.

She was silent for a minute, and we just stared at each other. She wiped away the few tears that escaped her eyes and started to speak again.

"Then we have finally come to an agreement on something, because I don't care either. I'm done. I'm done with this life, I'm done with your fucked-up-ass attitude, I'm done allowing you to blame me for shit you should really be praising me for, and I'm done with you! Cairo and I are leaving. I'll send him back here to visit you until you are able to come back to New York, but I'm not doing this with you anymore. I can't." She walked closer to me, bent down, and pressed her lips against mine.

The kiss lasted only a minute before she turned away and headed out of the room, leaving me alone with my thoughts and a fucked-up feeling coming over me.

Victoria

"When did you get back!" I dropped my bags and hugged Skye. Walking into the house from shopping, I was totally surprised to see her. I hadn't been updated since I left New York. It felt good having her back home. I finally would have someone to talk to about the nightmares I was having. I didn't feel in the least bit bad about killing Ariana, but it didn't stop her face from invading my thoughts while I tried to sleep. I shook off the eerie feeling I was starting to feel, focusing on the present.

"I got back a little while ago. Where are Ty and Pop Pop?" she questioned, looking past me to see if they were coming in.

"They coming. They're gathering all the bags to bring them inside. We went shopping, and I went ham for my nephew." I spoke excitedly, although I could see she wasn't in the mood. I just was really trying to pick her spirits up.

"You always do. I'm going to grab Cairo and lie down for a bit before I start packing our things," she said as she turned and walked away.

I was totally confused. Packing their things for what? I was going to get to the bottom of it and get the answers I wanted, but for now, I would give Skye the space she needed. I picked up my bags and headed up to my room to put them away.

As I sat on the edge of my bed unpacking the bags from the all-day shopping trip, I had an unsettled feeling in my stomach. I didn't want to talk to Skye because she seemed so upset when we did speak, so I decided to go talk to the second source. I walked out my bedroom and descended the steps, bypassing Ty and Pop Pop. I headed to Cameron's room. The door was slightly cracked, so I didn't see the point in knocking. I walked in and found him lying back on his bed with his arms across his eyes.

"Bro!" I said as I took a seat at the bottom of his bed.

He moved his arms from his eyes and sat up on the bed. "What up, kid. What you copped me from your little shopping spree?" he asked.

"Nothing," I said with a straight face even though I was lying.

"Ain't that some shit. Just spend up my money and not cop a nigga nothing," he said with a smirk on his face.

I laughed. He knew I was lying. Cam knew me like I knew myself. "You know I did punk shut up. But wassup with Skye? She said she was packing her and Cairo's things," I said, switching the conversation into serious mode.

"Oh. She was serious?" he asked.

"About what?" I was confused.

"We got into an argument. She said she was leaving and taking Cai, but I didn't really think she was for real," he said as hurt filled his expression.

"What were y'all arguing about now?" I needed to know how serious things had become between them. Their relationship was deteriorating at rapid speed, and it was painful to watch.

I listened to him give me the summary of their argument. As I expected, it was my brother's fault. He could be so stubborn at times, but I understood it because I was just like him. I felt kind of guilty that he was blaming her for getting locked up. He had no clue whatsoever that she did it to save me. I would have bet money that if he knew, he would feel differently about the situation. Skye was good to him. As a matter of fact, she was good to our family period. She didn't deserve the backlash she was receiving from Cam. Maybe things would be better if she just flat-out told him all that has transpired, help him better understand her methods and her reasoning. I still didn't quite understand why she thought it was a good idea to keep most of the things that had happened from Cam.

"Y'all gotta get it together. If not for y'all, for Cairo. This family been through too much already. When I say family, I include Hector and Pop Pop. A lot has happened, and they held this family down. I get that you're upset that your girl had to bear witness to some of the things that went down, but believe me when I tell you that everything Skye has done to date was necessary," I tried to explain to him. Knowing my brother, it went in one ear and other the other. He would come to terms with everything and accept it on his terms and his terms only.

"I really don't care about that. I just don't want her to take my son. Who knows when I'ma be cleared to go back to New York? I'm supposed to sit around here and not know how my son doing? Or see him when she feel like sending him? Nah, I'm not with that. If she wanna go, she can go ahead and leave Cai, though," he stated.

I just nodded. They both were stubborn as hell, but I knew they would get it together. The two of them were meant to be together.

"Well, bro, I don't know. I'ma talk to her and see where her head at. Let me go. I wanna shower and change before dinner," I said, getting up off the bed and leaving the room.

As I turned the corner to go up the stairs, I bumped into Ty.

Ty

"Where you rushing off to?" I asked Vic after kissing her on the forehead.

"I'm going to talk to Skye. I need to see what's up with her. She told Cam she's leaving and taking Cairo," Vic said.

I was shocked. I knew Skye was getting fed up with how Cam was acting toward her, but I didn't think she would get to the point where she would want to leave him, let alone take Cairo away from him.

"What you think talking to her going to do? You know once Skye sets her mind on something, it's a wrap," I said, pulling Vic closer to me.

"Stop, Ty. I know that, but I think if we all just sit down with Cam and just put everything on the table, he wouldn't act the way he does. Us keeping him in the dark about the things that have been going is just making matters worse."

Vic tried to get me to see how she viewed things, and I had to agree. The secrets were definitely piling on thick. When shit finally did hit the fan, it wasn't going to be nothing nice.

"I feel you, babe. If you can get Skye to agree to sit down with him and put him on, then I'm in, but I really do doubt she even trying to hear that," I retorted.

"I gotta give it a try. I mean, at least at the end of the day, if things don't work out, I can say I tried. Can you talk to Cam? See if he's up to it?" she asked, giving me the sexiest sad face I'd ever seen. She knew I wouldn't be able to tell her no. She was banking on that.

"You know what you're doing. But yeah, I got you. I'ma talk to my nigga now," I said, pulling her in for a kiss. Once we separated, I slapped her ass as she headed to go up the steps.

I walked down the corridor toward Cam's room. I honestly didn't know what I would say to my nigga. We hadn't really sat down and kicked it since last year. So much shit was going on, we never had the chance. Vic was right, though. It was time. I was all for laying shit on the table, but there was just one topic I wasn't open to discussing yet. I knocked on his door and waited for him to answer.

"Yo," Cam yelled from the other side of the door.

"What up, son? It's me. You dressed and shit?" I asked, not wanting to walk in on the nigga if he wasn't proper.

"Yeah, come in," Cam responded.

I turned the doorknob and walked into the room. "What up, bro," I said, taking a seat on the edge of his bed.

We slapped fives, and he gave me a nod. There was an awkward silence between us for a minute until I decided to break the silence.

"How's therapy and shit?" I asked, trying to get rid of the elephant that was standing smack dead in the center of the room.

"I'm here, so I don't have any complaints. Therapy is just therapy. Not where I wanna be, but far from where I started, so that's good right," he said, looking disinterested in the conversation.

I nodded. When he woke up from his coma, he couldn't even feel his legs. At least now he was able to maneuver around. Even if it was with a cane, it beat a wheelchair for life. I decided to kill the small talk and get straight to the point. It was either he was going to be down to sit with me and the ladies to discuss everything, or he wasn't. Straight like that.

"A'ight, I'm going to get to the point. You know a lot of shit has gone down since you been down. Some shit you know about, but most of it you don't," I began my mini speech.

I could see the look on his face go from complacent to angry as he cut me off. "Y'all been keeping shit from me? You out of all people? You supposed to be my nigga. Why y'all niggas acting like I'ma break into little pieces if y'all keep it one hundred with me? I'm a grown-ass man. I can handle this shit." He spoke with anger, which I was expecting. I would have felt the same way if the shoe were on the other foot.

"It wasn't even like that. If we told you half of the shit that went down, what would that have done? You would have been even more upset at the fact that there wasn't shit you could do about it. You already walking around here, acting like you carrying the weight of the world on your shoulders. Why would we even add to that? We had everything under control. If we didn't, you would have known." I explained the best way I could and just hoped that he understood.

"Real shit, I just wanna relax. Fuck all this talking. Skye wanna leave with Cairo, so be it. She better just make sure I see my son often. Niggas wasn't worried about talking to me before, and now y'all wanna powwow. I'm good on that. Y'all think this shit easy for me?" Cam stated.

He had a lot on his chest, so I sat there and listened. Cam was a nigga with pride, as most niggas were, but he took it to another level, which was why it shocked me to hear him tell me how he really felt about his condition. Cam was never the type to let anyone see him vulnerable, but there he was spilling his soul. I felt for him because I could see the eagerness he had in his eyes to get up and handle all the niggas who had wronged him. But by the same token, there was a look of defeat there.

"I hear you. I can't say that I understand what you going through, because I don't. What I do know is that you not alone. We got you. All this feeling sorry for yourself shit is wack. It's been a few months, and look at how much you progressed. You came out speaking like Cairo. Now look at you. You going to be a'ight, I guarantee that. I respect that you just wanna kick back right now, but sooner or later, we gotta talk," I stated, getting up from the bed. I walked out of the room because I knew Cam, and once he said he wasn't doing something, he wasn't going to change his mind until he was ready.

As I was heading up to Skye's room to talk to her and Vic, Adriana handed me Cairo, who was knocked out. I looked down at my godson while I walked up the steps, and in his face, I saw Cam. Skye's door was open, so I walked in and laid Cairo in the middle of her bed. Vic wasn't in there anymore, but I still stuck around and kicked it with Skye for a little bit.

I thought our relationship would have suffered after the shit that went down with Ari, but Skye really did forgive me like she said. She didn't hold it against me at all. That was mainly because Cairo was back, and he was safe. I just really hoped that once Cam found out, he would have the same attitude about it. I doubted it, but I was ready to roll with the punches. Whatever happened at that point was just going to happen.

Skye and I talked for a minute about her wanting to leave and go back to school. Even though I was on her side about going home and finishing school, I couldn't voice that. At the end of the day, Cam was still my brother, so instead of saying that I agreed, I just let her vent and get everything she needed to say off her chest. When she was done, I assured her that whatever happened with her and Cam, I was only a call away if she or Cai ever needed anything. After all the back and forth today, a nigga just wanted to kick back and relax. I left Skye alone with Cairo so I could do just that.

Chapter Eight

Skye

I was glad that Cameron wasn't in the mood to talk about everything, because honestly, neither was I. Sooner or later, I would have to come clean, but after our blowup earlier that day, I wasn't ready. My mind was on me getting my life back in order, moving back home with my baby, and getting back into school in August. Things wouldn't go back to normal overnight, but the same way I'd adjusted into this life, I planned to adjust back into my old way of doing things. I needed to be better for my son.

I glanced down next to me to my sleeping baby, who was smiling in his sleep. He must have been having a good dream. That made me smile. If it were up to me, my son would only know good times. He wouldn't have to endure none of the pain I did these last couple of months. My sole purpose at that point in time was to be the best me I could be for Cairo and make sure he was good. I intended to do that.

There was a light knock at my door, taking my attention away from my prince. I moved the pillows closer around him so he wouldn't roll, and I got off the bed to open the door. It was Pop Pop, the only person other than Cameron I just wasn't prepared to face.

"Hey, Pop Pop," I spoke as I reached out and hugged him.

"Hello, *nieta!*" he said, stepping into the room and closing the door behind him.

His warm smile turned into a frown, and I knew he too was there to chew me into pieces. Before he could even get to do that, I spoke up.

"Pop Pop, I know there is a lot we need to discuss, but can we talk later or tomorrow? I just want to lie down and rest with my son. I'm extremely fatigued," I said, hoping that he would understand and leave me be for a little while.

"I'll see you in the living room in fifteen minutes. If that's not enough time to gather your thoughts or what-ever you need to do, then I don't really know what to tell you," he spoke in a demanding tone before turning and leaving the room.

I should have known he wouldn't get it. I sighed and sat back on the bed. Cairo started to move around. He would be waking up soon. I went to pick him up just as his little eyes fluttered open. Scooping him up in my arms, I stared down at my future.

"Mommy loves you, Cairo. I promise I will make you proud," I said, kissing his hand before he broke out into tears.

"Fat man must be hungry," I spoke softly to him as I headed out of the room to make him a bottle.

I walked into the kitchen, and my mother already had a bottle ready. She knew he would be hungry when he woke up from napping. Even though we weren't seeing eye to eye at the moment, I couldn't deny that my mother had been extremely helpful with Cairo. I couldn't thank her enough for that.

"Give me him and go do what you need to do," she exclaimed while taking Cairo out of my arms.

I blew Cairo a kiss before turning and heading into the living room. I walked in to find Cameron, Ty, and Victoria sitting in complete silence.

Victoria

"Wassup, sis?" I asked when I realized Skye was standing in the doorway of the living room.

"Hey." She spoke dryly, walking toward me and sitting beside me.

No one attempted to speak first. I looked around at the three of them and knew I had to be the one to start the conversation.

"A'ight, no one wanted to sit down and put everything on the table, so I had to get Pop Pop to get y'all to come in here and talk. I see none of y'all wants to jumpstart the conversation, so I will," I stated right before taking a deep breath.

It only made sense to start from the beginning, so that's what I did. Cam had no idea how hard Skye took him being shot and going into a coma, so I put him on. Every day was a battle for her, not to mention she was pregnant and trying to keep it together for everyone. Of course, he felt like she had options, but I had to explain to him that there weren't any. The money my mother had in her accounts definitely would not have held us over in the event that Cam didn't wake up, so Skye made sure we had money. There was still ongoing beef that Skye set out to squash. I really didn't get the big deal. She was fine, Cairo was fine, the team was together and getting money. Wasn't that the end goal in the first place?

"You want me to accept that she did all that shit? You want me to look past the fact that she risked her life and the life of my son? Bet, Skye, it's all good. I'm over it,"

Cameron said, growing tired of the explanation I was trying to deliver to him.

"You can keep that. I don't care anymore, because clearly you still missing the point. I get that you would feel some type of way, but damn, I really don't deserve the shade. Like you said, though, it's all good," Skye said, leaning back against the couch as if she had said all she needed to say.

I took that little moment of silence as an opportunity to continue to mediate. I didn't feel like I was doing a good job at all, but anything was better than us walking around with unspoken tension.

"Y'all ready to tell me who kidnapped my fucking son and how the gangster over there got him back and ended up arrested, or is that shit still top secret?" Cam said before I was able to get my next point across.

I looked at Ty then at Skye. Neither one of them budged, so once again, I was left to give the explanation.

"Cairo was kidnapped by Ariana. Yeah, she was supposed to be dead, but whatever happened with that, she wasn't. She took Cairo, and once we found out she had him, Skye went to get him. You mad at her, but she got arrested protecting me. I shot and killed Ariana. Skye came up with a plan in like 2.5 seconds and got me out of there. If it weren't for her, I would be facing a murder charge right now. You been blaming her, and you didn't even know the half, Cam," I said, letting out a huge breath.

It felt good finally telling the truth about what happened. The looks on Ty's and Cam's faces were a mixture of disbelief and shock. There was another moment of silence before Cameron grabbed his cane, stood up, and exploded.

"You telling me because this nigga didn't have the balls to kill that bitch Ariana, my son was kidnapped and my sister had to commit her first murder?" he asked, taking a step toward Ty, who was now out of his seat as well.

"Yo, Cam, for real, chill," Ty stated, taking a stance, looking like he was ready for whatever.

"Fuck out of here. You telling me the pussy was that good?" Cam shouted, getting in Ty's face.

I took a step back because if they came to blows, I wasn't trying to catch a stray hook. Skye, on the other hand, wasn't trying to let that scene unfold like that. She jumped up from her seat and stood in between them.

"Cameron, stop blaming everyone for shit that happened. It happened. Let's move forward. This dude you ready to fight is the same dude who murdered his own father to save my life! Yeah, he messed up by not killing Ariana when he was supposed to, but you really think he would let her live for no apparent reason? Obviously, there's a reason everything happened the way it did. Come on now. You're too smart to be reacting so fucking stupid. Think! I'm done with this conversation. Get the fuck over it. Ty is family. He and Victoria are dating. You wanna scream, curse, and hit something, right? That's fucking stupid. He has been nothing but loyal to you, and he treats your sister the way she should be treated, so get the fuck over that too. I'm tired! Because you feel miserable, you want to make everyone else feel miserable too. Cut the shit, put on your big-man briefs, and get the fuck over this shit," Skye shouted before turning and walking out of the living room.

There was an intense stare down between Ty and Cam before Cam retreated to his room.

Cameron

When I got back to my room, I fell face-first into the bed. I had no idea shit unfolded the way Vic said. They were right. I really was taking my frustrations out on the wrong people. Ty really was my nigga. I couldn't think of one time when he wasn't there for me or did some shady shit in all the years we had known each other. Skye really had stepped up. Maybe I didn't want to accept it, because it wasn't what I wanted for her. When I met her, the main thing that attracted me to her, besides her being fine as fuck, was that she had plans for her life. Those plans didn't involve the streets, and I needed that. I'd had my share of street bitches, and I wanted different in the girl I would ultimately settle down with.

Her getting involved in my lifestyle was really only her doing what she had to do for me and my family. How could I not respect that? I had to. Vic didn't surprise me as much. She'd been voicing how badly she wanted no part of the business, but as long as I was able, she would never taste this life, let alone catch a body. Thinking about Vic killing Ari brought me back to Skye. She was ready to take a murder charge to protect my sister. She was indeed the most selfless person I had ever encountered. You don't come across people like that very often, so I knew I had to get my shit straight and find a way to get her back. The last thing I wanted to do was to lose half of me, and that's exactly what Skye was.

I couldn't be mad at Ty and Vic dating, because I had a feeling it would happen. Ty used to make jokes back in the day about Vic being the girl he would marry, but I always took him half serious. When he was serious about a chick, he was a good dude, so I wasn't worried about him hurting her. If anything, it would have been the other way around.

Ty killed Jeff? I really did miss a lot. How did that even present itself? I was sure he wasn't left with an option, but I knew that he wasn't taking the decision he made too well. Jeff wasn't a saint, and he definitely had vices, but that was his pops at the end of the day. It was really time for me to accept that if I didn't have anyone else in the world, I had my sister, Skye, and Ty. They proved that they had me no matter what.

After that night, Skye kept her word when she said she was leaving with Cairo. I tried to protest, but she wasn't having it. There was nothing I could do to get her to change her mind, and although I still needed therapy, I couldn't be away from my son, or Skye for that matter. It took some convincing, but my mother gave in, and a few days after Skye left, we were headed back to New York as well. My mother found me a therapist who would be coming to the house five times a week to help me continue my progress. I was cool with that as long as I was just a car ride away from Cairo and Skye versus a plane ride.

The first few weeks back were cool. I saw my son every day and kicked it with Pop Pop often. He had become much more than just Skye's grandfather. Pop Pop taught me a lot of shit I thought I knew but really had no idea about. It was cool. He was like a mentor or some shit. As far as the team was concerned, it was business as usual. Pop Pop kept providing the work, and my niggas kept getting it off. To their knowledge, though, I was still away. I would have loved to see my team, but in the event that shit popped off, I needed to be one hundred. I used my cane less but still needed it from time to time. Until I was straight, it was best if everyone thought I was still low, recuperating.

Chapter Nine

Victoria

I missed Miami, but I couldn't lie and say that it didn't feel good to be back home. I missed having Cairo and Skye around every day, but it was okay. I got to see them almost every day. Cam was in a better space and getting stronger every day. The more he improved, the more the old Cam started to resurface. Ty and I were doing great. Once Cam got over the initial shock of us being together, we told my mother, and she accepted it. She loved Ty, so I knew she wouldn't mind us being together as long as he treated me well, and that he did.

The doorbell rang and took my attention away from the movie. I looked and saw that no one else was going to budge, so I had to get up and get it. I was mad, because *Rush Hour* was one of my favorite movies. The quicker I got the door, the quicker I could get back to the movie. I got up from leaning on Ty and headed toward the front door.

When I opened it, I was confused because there was a woman on the other side of the door, one I had never seen a day in my life.

"Hey, can I help you?" I asked, waiting for her to introduce herself or tell me why she was on my property.

"Hi, I'm Sandra. Is Cameron or Mariah here?" she asked in a polite manner.

"One sec." I closed the door and headed back into the family room, where everyone was completely wrapped up in the movie.

"Mom and Cam, there's a lady named Sandra asking for the two of you," I announced.

"What the hell is she doing at my house?" my mother yelled. Her outburst shocked me. She rarely lost her cool like that, which made me even more interested in finding out who this Sandra character was.

"Let her in, sis," Cam said, much calmer than my mom.

I headed back to the door and opened it to find her still standing there. I motioned for her to come in, and I led her into the living room.

"Hello, Mariah. Hi, everyone." Sandra said as she stepped into the living room.

All eyes were now on her. My mother was eyeing her suspiciously, but Cam seemed cool.

"Don't hello me. You have nerve coming to my house, Sandra," my mother said, getting up from her seat.

"Mom, relax. How do you know her anyway?" Cam asked, just as confused as I was.

"I knew every bitch your father cheated on me with. I wasn't dumb. Sandra was my friend, though, until she showed up here pregnant with your fucking brother," my mother blurted out.

Realizing the last bit of information was too much, she put her hand over her mouth in an "oops, that wasn't supposed to come out" manner. At least now I knew who she was. She was Matthew's mother. Why the hell was she at our house? I hoped she wasn't coming to ask for money, because I was sure my mother wouldn't think twice about beating the brakes off her up and down the driveway. I knew that by the look she was giving her.

"Mariah, I told you Hassan was not Matthew's father. Yes, I did sleep with him, but he did not father my child.

I don't know what else I can say to get you to believe that. I really didn't come here to hash it out over things we can't change. Jeff knew that he was Matthew's father but refused to tell Hassan. If you want to blame anyone for thinking your husband had a baby on you, blame him. He could have put the rumors to rest. He had DNA results to prove it. I'm just looking for Matthew. I know that he and Cameron stayed in touch, but I haven't heard from him. He hasn't been to Atlanta? I'm just worried. I didn't have any of your numbers, but I knew I could find someone here," Sandra spoke, not realizing that the bomb she had dropped had us all ready to pass out.

I looked over to the one I knew would be affected the most and saw all the color fade from his skin. He had chocolate skin, but he turned dry, as if all the rich chocolate had been drained from his body. I walked over to Ty and put my hand on his shoulder, and he pushed it away from him before getting up and walking out of the living room.

As I walked out behind him, I heard Cameron telling Sandra that we hadn't heard from Matthew either and that he would contact her if we did. I knew that was a lie. Matthew was in someone's dirt, napping.

I caught up with Ty leaning against the fountain that rested in our circular driveway. He tried to send me back into the house, telling me that he needed a minute alone, but I couldn't grant him that. He was hurting, and as his girl, it was my job to carry that hurt with him. I stood in front of him in silence. When he was ready, he would speak to me. I just wanted him to know that I was there for him.

"The last person in the world who shared my blood is dead, and because of me at that. I killed the only two niggas in the world who were my family." He spoke through the tears that flowed freely from his eyes.

He had been hurting over having to kill his father. He never wanted to talk about it. It was the one topic that was off-limits no matter what. I knew that it was only a matter of time before he got tired of walking around with that baggage and let it out. Hearing that Matthew was indeed his brother sent him over the edge. I could even pretend to understand the way he was feeling. How would I have felt if I had to kill my mother and my brother? Ty's dad and Matthew really did deserve their deaths, but Ty didn't deserve to live with the guilt of delivering their death sentences.

"I have nobody, Vic! My own mother walked out on me. I probably walked right on by her and didn't even know who she was. I don't have grandparents, no other siblings. I killed my pops. I killed my brother. I will never have family."

I had no idea what to say to him. I just wanted to hold him and tell him everything would be okay, so that's what I did. I pulled him closer to me and wrapped my arms around him.

"It's going to be okay, baby. I'm here for you. No matter what, you will have family. You have us, and that will never change," I told him while I rubbed his back.

"Nah, that's your fam. Yeah, I'm treated like family, but it doesn't change that nobody in there shares my blood."

I took a step back from him and stared intensely in his eyes. I was so in love with him that sometimes I couldn't comprehend it. I lifted his hand and placed it on my stomach.

"No. You will always have us." I cracked a half smile in hopes that he understood what I was telling him.

He looked like he got it but wasn't really sure.

"You're going to be a dad," was all I was able to get out before he lifted me off the ground and kissed me.

I knew that in the back of his mind, he was still thinking about Jeff and Matthew, but at least in the forefront, he could focus on the baby we would be bringing into the world together.

He didn't know that I been in touch with a private investigator, trying to contact his mom. I didn't want to tell him until everything was set in stone. I didn't want to get his hopes up just to let him down. So focusing on me and our baby was the right thing to do for the time being. The baby would forever love him and always be his blood.

He was anxious to know when I'd found out, so I explained to him about having Skye go with me to the doctor when I was over at her house visiting Cairo. He was so happy, and I was so happy that I could put a smile on his face during a time when he was hurting.

While we stood there embracing each other, I thought back to the day I found out I was pregnant.

I was over at Skye's, spending some time with her. I had a feeling I was pregnant because my menstrual hadn't come twice, and it always came. Since I'd first gotten it at age 13, there wasn't a month that it didn't. Even if my cycle changed, it would come early or late, but it always came. I was nervous and knew that I could talk to Skye about anything, so I did just that. She was so happy.

"Let's go to the doctor right now. I hope you are. Cairo needs a playmate," Skye joked as she started putting on her sneakers.

She was serious about going to the doctor that very minute. Even though I told her we would have to wait forever since we were walking in, she still said we were going. So we did. The entire time we waited, I bit my nails. I was so nervous. I had become so adjusted to the thought of being a mother. I was ready, and if I wasn't pregnant, I would have been sad.

We were finally called back, I thought I was going to have a panic attack due to how nervous and anxious I was. I couldn't focus on anything other than getting the results. Once everything was over, we waited.

"Congratulations. You are going to be a mommy." My doctor spoke the words I wanted to hear, and in that moment, something changed. It was no longer about just me. I was going to be a mother. I couldn't wait to meet my prince or princess, and I couldn't wait to tell Ty. I knew he would be happy. I just wanted the time to be perfect.

"I still can't believe that nigga was my blood," Ty spoke into my ear, bringing me back to the present and reminding me where we were.

"It's the past, baby. I know you carry guilt about your dad and now you will because of Matthew, but there is so much more to look forward to," I verbalized, hoping that he would let it go. I couldn't relate because I wasn't in his shoes, but I didn't want him walking around moping about something he couldn't change.

He smiled and kissed me again before we headed back into the house. As we were heading in, Sandra was leaving. She apologized to us for interrupting and asked once again to have Matthew contact her if we spoke to him. Ty's eyes fell to the floor as he told her he would, knowing that he couldn't grant her that. Her son was gone forever.

Cameron

I was waiting in the foyer for Skye to pull up. The bomb Sandra dropped really shook shit up, and I knew Ty was feeling some way. I made a mental note to talk to him about it later. At that moment, the focus was on Cairo. I couldn't wait to see my son. Not having him in the same house with me every day was harder than I thought it would be. I got to see him whenever I wanted, which was often every day, even if it was just for a minute, but it wasn't the same.

When I saw her truck come to a complete stop, I walked out of the house so I could help her. She stepped out of the truck, looking fine as fuck. She didn't even have to try hard. She wore her hair in loose curls, which bounced with every movement she made. I smiled at her, and she smirked back. I knew she still wanted me, but she was just as stubborn as I was. She wasn't going to give in that easy.

"What up, baby mother?" I said as I kissed her forehead and headed to open the back door to get Cai out of his car seat.

"Hello, baby father," she said with a chuckle. I hated her calling me that just as much as she hated me calling her baby mother.

"Cai, look at you. You getting big, man," I said, holding Cairo in my arms.

"Stop being dramatic. You just saw him yesterday." Skye laughed, grabbing his baby bag.

We walked up to the house side by side like it should always be. When we got inside, Skye walked off. I assumed she was going to say her hellos since everybody was home. Cairo and I, on the other hand, headed straight up to my room, where I took off his clothes. He was in the crib for the day, so he was straight in just his onesie. I was in the process of taking off my kicks when Skye and Vic came in.

"Dang, you just going to hold him hostage?" Victoria said as she bent down and picked Cairo up off the bed.

"Nah, I just wanted to get him comfortable. You can take him to see Ma. I'll be down there in a minute," I said, kicking off my second sneaker.

"Come on, big boy," Vic said, turning and walking out of the room. She closed the door behind her.

I looked up at Skye as she was unzipping her jacket. She made the simplest gesture look sexy as fuck.

"Why you staring at me?" she said, putting her hand on her hip.

"I can't admire my BM beauty?" I let out with a laugh. That would piss her off a little.

"I hate when you call me that." She pouted.

I stood up and walked over to her. I placed each of my hands on her hips and pulled her close. She moved her head back and gave me a look that said she wanted me to let her go, but that wasn't going to happen. I leaned forward and kissed her. At first, she was hesitant, but I felt her body give in to me as she returned my kiss with passion.

I moved my hands from her hips to the bottom of her shirt and slowly raised it and pulled it over her head. I slowly moved my hands up her back and unhooked her bra.

"Please stop. I don't want to go there with you," Skye's mouth said, but the racing of her heart and the shortness of her breath were singing another song.

I took one of her titties into my mouth and gently pinched the nipple of the other. My dick was extremely hard and threatening to break free from my basketball shorts any minute. Without releasing the hold my mouth had on her titty, I reached down and undid her jeans. They were skintight, so it took me a minute to wiggle them over her hips, which had seemed to spread after she'd given birth. I had to thank my boy. He did his mother's body right. Everything on her was enhanced. Her boobs were bigger but not saggy, her ass was fatter, and I bet the pussy was better.

Once her jeans hit her ankles, she stepped out of them. All talk of wanting me to stop went out the window the minute her jeans came off. I rubbed her washboard-flat stomach, which had no visible signs that she had given birth a few months back, and trailed my hand down to her box. Moving her thong to the side, I slid two fingers into her, feeling her juices flow over my fingers, which let me know she was ready.

I removed my fingers and sucked them before picking her up and tossing her on the bed. I quickly came out of my ball shorts and briefs, freeing my piece. I walked over to the bed and slid between her legs, stopping when I came face-to-face with her pussy. I reached up and pulled her down by her thighs and met her opening with my tongue. The initial contact made her squirm. She hadn't been sucked or fucked in a minute, so I knew she was anticipating this even if she wouldn't admit it.

I stuck my tongue deeper inside her box and came out quick, repeating that motion over and over. She was tryin'a shove my head closer to her. I wasn't having it, though. I was gonna make her tell me she wanted it.

"'Tell me that the pussy is mine,'" I sang out in the best imitation of Miguel that I could do. She said nothing, so I entered her with two fingers and flicked my tongue across her clit.

"A'ight, fuck it," I said, sitting up.

"Pleaseeee, Cameron. I want to feel you. I need to feel you," she moaned out.

That's all I wanted. She didn't need to ask twice. I dove in headfirst and tongue fucked her brains out. With each lashing I gave her clit with my tongue, I felt the walls she had built break down. I stuck two fingers back inside her pulsating pussy and fingered her while I gently nibbled her clit. Her body temperature was rising, and I felt the heat radiating from her. The grip she had on my head tightened, and her legs locked around my neck. Her body trembled as she released a river flow of her juices.

I caught it all as if I were drinking from a faucet. Her body went limp, and she sank deeper in the memory-foam mattress. I wasn't done with her yet, though. Using one hand, I flipped her over on her stomach and pulled her up by her thighs. I admired the view of her face down, ass up. With one hand, I grabbed a handful of her curls and pulled her toward me while I used my other hand to lead my piece to her opening.

"Why are you doing this to me?" Skye yelled out in bliss as she tightened the grip she had on the sheets.

Ignoring her pleas, I dug deeper into her cave. I wanted her to feel my shit in her chest, and by the way she was trying to get away, I knew I accomplished just that. I pulled her back toward me and went in deeper, and she clenched her walls around my dick. That shit drove me absolutely crazy. I thrust in and out faster, going deeper each time. Skye was meeting my thrusts and throwing her shit right back at me. I felt my shit about to explode, so I went harder and let off my nut deep inside her. I didn't pull out until my shit was drained.

I rolled onto my back, and without me having to say a word, Skye climbed on top of me and slid down on my semi-hard dick. As soon as my shit felt the tightness of her pussy, it got rock hard again. I looked up at Skye while she bit down on her bottom lip and bounced on my shit mercilessly. I gripped her by her waist and held her in place while I pumped in and out of her. Each stroke made her moans intensify.

Neither of us was worried about being heard. I pulled her down so her titties were against my chest, and I kissed her as Skye rode my dick.

"I love you, Skye," I managed to get out in between kisses.

She reached up and held on to the top of the leather headboard and went up, down, and round and round all on my joystick. I felt another nut building up, but I wanted her to cum with me. I rolled over, still inside her, and raised her legs up to her head. Shorty's toes were damn near touching her neck.

"Oh my . . . Shiiiit, Cameron," she yelled out.

She was on the verge of cumming, so I went harder and at a faster pace. Her body trembled beneath me just as I let off another load of my men in her pussy. I owned that whether Skye liked that thought or not. I stayed in her shit 'til her convulsions ceased. I leaned over and kissed her, pulled out, and rolled over on my back next to her.

"I love you too, Cameron," she finally said.

I let that linger while we both caught our second wind.

Skye

I got up off the bed and started to put my clothes back on. I wanted to shower badly, but I wanted to get away from Cameron just as badly. Not because I didn't love him or didn't want to be with him. Definitely not because the sex wasn't great, because it was impeccable. But because Cameron needed to realize that in order for us to move forward with our relationship, he had major changes to make. He needed to understand that he couldn't persuade me with great sex. Did it help? Yes. Did it lighten my mood? Absolutely! However, it didn't mend our relationship, and until he fully comprehended that, our relationship status would remain what it was. We were Cairo's parents, nothing more, nothing less.

I was standing there in my jeans and bra when Cameron finally decided to speak. "You just going to leave?" he asked with hurt behind his eyes.

Through the time of us being together, I'd learned him like I knew myself. I knew when he was hurt. I knew when he was sad, frustrated, tired, hungry. Shit, I even knew when he needed to take a shit. He was my love, there was no denying that, but I wanted more. I needed more. Cairo had to see me getting more from him so he would know exactly how to treat his woman when the time came.

"Yes. I told you I didn't want to go there, Cameron. We can't get past our problems by covering them up with the sheets. We really need to work at being a couple again," I said, slipping my shirt back over my head. I felt my hair. It was disheveled and all over the place. I did my best by patting it down, and then I slipped my arms into my coat.

"I'll call you when I get home," I said before blowing him a kiss and heading out of the room.

When I got downstairs, I walked to the living room to say goodbye to everyone and to kiss my son. All eyes were on me. They knew what was going on upstairs between me and Cameron. I played it off, though. I gave out hugs before kissing Cairo and heading out to my truck.

In the safety of my car, I let out a sigh. I missed Cameron so much, more than I was willing to admit. I wanted to jump out of the car and run right back into his arms, but I had to put my foot down. A guy would only do to a female what she allowed, and the way Cameron acted toward me when he'd gotten out of his coma wasn't going to cut it. He had to come correct if he wanted us to be the family we were supposed to be. Sooner or later, he would get it right. I wasn't going to stress. At that time, things were going fine. I wanted to enjoy it before the next storm hit.

I pushed the button on my key fob, and the car came to life. I couldn't wait to get home to shower and just relax. I missed Cairo whenever he was staying the night with his dad, but I couldn't say I didn't enjoy the quiet.

When I pulled up to my building, I drove into the residential parking area and parked my truck. I climbed out of the truck and dug into my bag to retrieve my vibrating phone. I looked down and saw that it was Cameron. As I slid to my finger across the screen to answer, someone grabbed my arm, forcing me to turn around.

"What the fuck? Get off me!" I shouted as I realized it was JR.

"Chill, chill. I just want to talk to you, that's it," JR said, letting my arm go.

"You had to stake out the parking garage waiting for my return just to talk to me?" I said, backing up a little. I knew I would have to face JR sooner or later, but I didn't think much of it since he wasn't going to jail. There was no murder weapon, so the case went cold. Hopefully he just wanted answers and not problems.

"You hard to catch up with. The few times I did see you, you had Cairo. I wasn't trying to step to you while you had your kid," he said, taking a step toward me.

"I can hear you. You don't need to get close to me to talk. Wassup?" I said, growing impatient and wishing I had a gun on me. I would have dropped him where he stood.

"I just want to know what happened that day at my crib. How did you know Ariana and I were there? Why did you shoot her and leave me to take the fall for it?" he said, looking to his left then back at me.

He was the epitome of suspect at that point. I felt like either he wanted to kill me or he was wired and was trying to get me locked up. Neither was going to happen that day. I was sure of that. I had to play my cards right. I was a law student whose career was going to be talking people out of sticky situations. I was sure I could get myself out of that. I was also sure that JR had to be dealt with as soon as possible.

"Her mother told me she was at your house, JR. I went there to whoop her ass because she dragged my baby into our drama. But that was it. I didn't get a good look at the person who shot her. We were tussling, and she was on top of me. I heard a gun go off, and when I felt safe enough to move, the person was gone." I'd lied through my teeth and lied so well that I almost believed it myself.

"I don't believe you, Skye. You like my sis. You could keep it a hundred with me," he spoke as he started pacing back and forth.

"You right, we are like brother and sister, which is why I would never leave you to face a murder charge. I was a suspect, and so were you. My mother advised me to stay low and not communicate with anyone until everything blew over. I'm sorry how everything played out, but look on the bright side. You aren't locked up, are you? Let it go and move on with your life like I'm trying to do," I stated calmly, taking another step away from him.

He mumbled a few words under his breath and turned to walk away. I scurried to the elevator and placed the phone to my ear once I realized Cameron had been on the line the entire time.

"Hello," I said into the phone once I was in the safety of the elevator.

"Ty and I are in the car on our way. When you get upstairs, make sure your door is locked, and stay by your phone. I'll be there in a minute," Cameron barked into the phone before ending the call.

As I stepped into my place, I closed the door behind me and secured all the locks. I couldn't focus on anything except that if JR wanted me dead, he had the perfect opportunity. I didn't like the feeling that I was that accessible. It was time for me to move, especially now, since I had Cairo. I didn't feel safe in my own home, and I wasn't going to live like a prisoner. I sat on the couch in the living room with my knees pulled into my chest. I took advantage of the silence and gathered my thoughts while I waited for Cameron.

Chapter Ten

Cameron

Fuck not being ready to hit the streets. The minute a nigga thought it was okay to approach Skye where she rested her head was the exact minute it was time for me to tie up every loose end that was left. I was able to get around without my cane, so I was straight. The rest of my healing had to be done on the move. I would continue my physical therapy because I didn't want any setbacks, but I was done sitting around the crib. If niggas wanted to see Cam back in action, their wish was my command.

"What made the nigga JR think he could press Skye and not have to deal with ramifications?" Ty said, pissing me off all over again.

"These niggas really be forgetting, son. Has it been that long?" I asked. It was a rhetorical question, though, and Ty knew that, so he said nothing and continued to drive.

When we finally got to Skye's crib, Ty found a parking spot, and we hurried upstairs to her apartment. I rang the bell and announced that it was me so she would keep calm. As soon as she opened the door, I pulled her into me for a hug and stepped inside with Ty right behind me.

"You good?" I asked her, although she appeared fine.

"Yes," she uttered and walked back toward the living room.

As I followed her, I cursed out loud about JR being brave, pressing her at her spot. I didn't know where she got all the strength she possessed, but she was really one of the strongest people I knew. She barely let niggas see her sweat, but I knew she was pissed.

"I really think he was wearing a wire or something," Skye said as I sat down beside her.

"It don't matter. That nigga should have left well enough alone. When I get through with him, he going to wish he did," I shouted.

"What's the plan?" Ty asked, coming from the kitchen with a bottle of water in his hand.

"Y'all don't have to do anything. I got this one," Skye said, causing me to look at her crazy.

She sensed that I was confused by her statement and went on to explain herself. Skye never told us about her and Vic getting JR's prints on the gun Vic used to kill Ariana until that moment. She said they figured the fewer people who knew about the gun, the better the chances it would work if the time presented itself. Skye didn't even have a clue where the gun was located. She wanted it that way. Her being alert and my seeing how she handled certain situations really made it easier for me to come to terms with the things that had happened while I was in the coma.

Skye really did know what she was doing. She was the smartest of us all, because all her moves were calculated to a T. Rarely did she act on impulse, and that's what kept her alive and out of jail. Niggas in the game could definitely learn a lot from her. I couldn't even front. Shorty had me cheesing hard as hell as she broke down how she planned on using the gun against JR. At first she didn't want to do it, and there really wasn't a need for her to. She and JR were both off the hook. No gun, no case. He had to fuck it all up by pressing it, and now he was going to pay the ultimate price.

"Damn, sis, that was a smooth-ass plan. How your ass get so hip to this shit?" Ty asked, acknowledging that it was indeed a good plan.

Skye smiled and leaned her head on my shoulder. I rubbed her cheek and told her I loved her. Together or not, I didn't really see myself not loving her. We'd been through so much in such a short period of time, and instead of packing up and running for the hills, she'd stuck it out with a nigga. How could I not love her? Not to mention, she gave me Cairo.

"I'll handle it from here, Skye. I'll get the location of the gun from Vic and get it to that nigga Detective Harris. You won't have to worry about JR. In the meantime, I think you should move back into the Long Island crib, and I think you need to look into getting a gun license. It's a process, but I'd rather you have a legal piece on you at all times than some illegal shit and you get caught up on a gun charge," I explained.

Skye wasn't feeling the idea of moving back into my house, but she compromised and said she would go stay at her grandfather's crib on Staten Island. Of course I would have rather had her laid up at my crib with me, but her getting out of this spot that niggas knew of was better than nothing.

"I'm going to take a shower. Can you stay the night with me?" Skye asked as she got up from the couch.

"Yeah, I'll stay. Cairo's with Mom anyway. Let me kick it with Ty for a minute," I replied.

Skye said bye to Ty before heading to the room for a shower.

"How you want to handle this, son?" Ty asked once Skye was out of earshot.

"When you get back to the house, find out from Vic where the gun at. After that, we will pay that nigga JR a visit. I'ma body him but leave the gun behind. Let the pigs bury him and the case at the same damn time," I said, leaning back against the couch.

Ty agreed that it was a solid plan and said he would hit me up once he got the location on the murder weapon. After he headed out and I locked the door behind him, I went and joined Skye in the shower.

Chapter Eleven

Man

It felt good to be back. A nigga missed the life. Sitting back with a shit bag attached to me wasn't how I wanted to spend the rest of my life. It was music to my ears when my doctor announced that I was getting the shit removed. Only thing I could think about was hitting the streets and getting back to the money. While I was down, my niggas stayed low. They couldn't afford any run-ins with Cam's boys until I was up and ready to pop off. Unfortunately, that gave them fuck boys the chance to slide in and take over my blocks. I wasn't too concerned about that, though, because I was back and ready to go hard.

I was a little fucked up when I found out Ari got bodied. I knew it was coming, though. She was reckless and always on some other shit, so shorty was bound to slip up. I was more tight that I didn't have a source anymore. There were other ways to get information, but the way shorty ran her mouth made shit much easier for me. I had a few tricks up my sleeve and couldn't wait to put them into effect.

I stepped out of the cab as it came to a complete stop in front of my house. Nobody knew I would be home today. I wanted my return to be a surprise to everyone. As I walked toward my crib, I heard someone calling my name.

"Yo, Man," the voice called out.

I turned around and spotted my nigga O jogging up the block. When he reached me, I dapped him up. O was my brother like my mother's kids, like the nigga Hov said. I had mad love for him because he always had my back. It didn't matter what it was. He was always ready and proved himself to be loyal on many occasions.

"What up," I said, leaning against the gate that surrounded my building.

"Shit, why you ain't let us know you was coming back to the hood today?" O questioned while he pulled out a Black & Mild.

"Just wanted to pop up, ya know. What's been up?" I questioned, already knowing the answer.

As expected, he told me all the shit I already knew. It was time for Cam and Ty to take that one-way trip to the crossroads. All this back-and-forth shit was getting wack. I just wanted to stack my bread, fuck bitches, and live comfortably. I couldn't do that peacefully with them niggas still breathing the same air as me.

"I hear you. I'm back, though, and I'm ready to lay them niggas down for good and get back to this paper. Feel me?" I stated as we slapped fives, signaling we were on the same page.

"You already know that whatever the plan is, count a nigga in. I got a li'l shorty to feed," he said, taking a pull of the Black.

"Word. Speaking of which, how your daughter doing?" I asked.

"Getting big and bad as fuck," O replied.

We shared a laugh and walked around the gate to the entrance of my building. As we were walking into the building, my cousin and her homegirl were coming out. I hadn't seen her in a minute, so I was shocked.

"What up, big head!" I shouted, pulling her in for a hug.

"Hey, cuz. Auntie didn't tell me you were coming home today. It's good to see you up and doing well," my cousin said, giving me and O a once-over.

"She didn't know, but yeah, it's good to see you too. What you doing out here?" I asked.

"Visiting for a bit. You know I had to stop by to check on your mom. I gotta go, though. Man, call me. The number is still the same," she said before hugging me and making her exit.

As she walked away, a light bulb went off, forcing a smile on my face. Shit was about to be over real soon.

Ty

The sun peeked through the curtains and did a dance routine on my face, forcing me to open my eyes. Vic's leg was draped across me, and her head was on my chest. I looked down at her and smiled, thinking about the crazy-ass sex session we'd had the night before. The thought of it made my dick hard. I contemplated starting my day by taking a dip in her box, but I knew I had other shit that needed to be handled. I kissed her forehead before sliding out of bed.

"Where are you going?" she asked with her eyes still closed.

So much for not waking her up.

"My bad, baby. I didn't want to wake you up. I'm about to shower and shit. I gotta head out and handle some shit with Cam," I said, walking toward the bathroom until I remembered I needed something else from her. "Yo, Vic, where you stashed that gun?"

My question caught her off guard, because the look on her face was a mixture of being busted and confused. She let the question marinate before finally answering me.

I was shocked at the response she gave. When did she and Skye learn all these tactics and shit they were using? Shorty had hidden the gun in the nigga's backyard. Yeah, it was reckless going back to the crime scene, but at the same time, it was smart as hell. If the location did get out, it would still fall on JR. I nodded at her and smiled before going into the bathroom to shower and shit.

When I got out of the shower, Vic was curled up in a fetal position, asleep. I really must have worn her out the previous night. Shit, I was still tired myself, but getting at the nigga JR was important. I quickly got dressed in a Vinnies Styles crewneck and a pair of Trues and slipped on my wheat construction Timberlands. I kissed Vic before heading to Cam's room to get him changing clothes and dipping.

For the entire drive to Skye's crib, I hoped that Cam was really up to putting in work. It'd been a minute, and he still had his physical therapy sessions and shit. I just wasn't convinced that he was ready. It was too late, though. There was no turning back or changing his mind. In the event that he wasn't ready, all I could do was hold my nigga down like I had been doing.

As I pulled up to Skye's building, a Charger was pulling out, freeing up a parking spot. I pulled in as soon as there was enough space. I hated having to park blocks away and walking down, so the spot was clutch. After parking, I killed the engine and headed upstairs.

Skye

I erotically threw my head back and clenched my eyes shut. I leaned back on the counter, putting all my weight on my hands, and ground forward to meet Cameron's thrust. What started out as making something to eat had turned into a hot and steamy sex intermission. I didn't have any complaints, though.

"Oh my . . ." I moaned out as Cameron hit my spot repeatedly.

There was knock out my front door. I was almost totally oblivious to it, and I blocked it out. I was too close to going over the edge.

"Damn, babe!" Cameron grunted as he thrust in and out harder and faster.

I tightened the grip my legs had on his waist as I felt my climax building. The knocking was persistent. They either had to wait or go away.

"Fuckkk, Cameron!" I screamed as my body convulsed and released all over his manhood.

The pulsating of my walls sent Cameron over the edge too. He pulled me close and released his men inside me. We took a few minutes to catch our breath before Cameron leaned forward and kissed me, playfully biting my lip. I'd totally forgotten about the visitor at the door until I heard the knock again.

"Who the fuck is that?" Cameron asked, looking at me sideways.

"I don't know," I said, jumping off the counter. I pulled my robe close around me and tied it before heading into the foyer to get the door.

"Who?" I asked as I approached the door.

"Finally, sis. Open the door."

I immediately recognized the voice as belonging to Ty. I open the door, and he playfully mushed me. "Y'all niggas really can't stay off each other," Ty said in between laughs.

He knew what he'd walked in on, so I didn't need to respond. I let out a low chuckle before closing and locking the door once he was inside.

"Make yourself at home. Your boy will be out after his shower," I stated.

"A'ight. Here, I brought the nigga some clothes. I know he don't have no up-to-date shit here," Ty said, handing me the bag that housed Cameron's change of clothes.

I took the bag from Ty and headed to my bedroom. I heard the shower running, so I opened my robe, let it fall to the floor, and joined Cameron in the shower.

"Cameron, I love you," I declared.

Cameron turned to face me and pulled me close to him. "I really am sorry for everything. You have been nothing but the glue that my family . . . no, that I needed to keep everything together, and I appreciate that. We are not where I want us to be in terms of our relationship, and I take the blame for that completely. We will get there, though, I promise you, and when we do, it will be better than it was. I love you and Cairo more than anything in the world, baby girl. If you don't know anything else, know that." Cameron replied before leaning down and kissing me.

No more words needed to be shared. We took turns washing each other off and then exited the shower. Once we were in the bedroom, I gave him the bag of clothes Ty had bought over, and we both got dressed.

"Babe, I gotta run out with Ty and handle some shit. Cairo is at home with Ma and Vic. I really don't want you staying here, so you should head to Staten Island or go to my house," Cameron said as he stood in the doorway, ready to go.

"Don't worry about me. You be careful. If you start feeling weak or anything, please go home. Don't be reckless. You have our son to think about," I said in a serious tone.

Cameron nodded at me, letting me know that he acknowledged what I said to him, before walking toward me, planting a kiss on my forehead, and leaving. I was worried. Actually, that was an understatement for how I felt. Cameron and Ty were out for blood, and I just wished they'd use the gun to get him locked up. That's all that was needed. Feeling the need to vent, I grabbed my phone and immediately called Victoria.

"Hey, sis," Victoria said, answering the phone on the first ring.

"What you doing?" I inquired.

"I just finished getting dressed. What's wrong? You sound stressed. What'd my brother do now?" Victoria asked as if she just knew it was related to Cameron.

I informed her that he hadn't done anything to me per se, before giving her a rundown on how I was feeling. No matter what, Victoria would side with me. She, too, was worried about the men and wished they just took the easy way out. That wasn't in their DNA, though. JR was bound to get dealt with in a barrage of gunfire. It's just the way Ty and Cameron handled things.

"Don't worry about it. That damn murder looming over us going to die today with JR," Victoria stated with venom dripping from her tone. She'd answered the phone so cheerfully and switched up her demeanor that quick. She and Cameron were definitely related. I really hoped that she was sitting this one out. I badly wanted a part of it, but it was important to me that I kept my promise to God.

"Let them handle it," I stated, hoping she would let go of whatever thoughts came to her mind.

"I love you. I will let them handle it because I know they got this. I also know that when they catch him, it's a wrap, so breathe easy. I gotta go, though," Victoria said before ending the phone call.

I let out a huge sigh before falling back on my bed. It just was a never-ending cycle. It was always something!

The shit was never going to end. I was completely convinced.

Victoria

After hanging up with Skye, I grabbed my car keys and headed outside to my whip. I wanted to kick it with her more—shit, I wanted nothing more than to be by her side while Cam and Ty handled JR—but I had something else on my plate. I was running late for my meeting and couldn't get sidetracked. For the past few weeks, I had been working with a private investigator. I was hoping to find any bit of information on Ty's mother. I'd watched him hurt over not having her or his father, and it killed me. I promised myself that I would do all that I could to reunite them. I didn't plan on stopping until there were absolutely no options left.

I pulled up to Amy Ruth's in Harlem, where I was scheduled to meet with my PI. Lucky for me, there was a parking spot right out front. I threw the car into park before jumping out and heading inside. I browsed through the patrons in search of the familiar face. I spotted him sitting in the back of the restaurant, and I headed in his direction. When he felt my presence, he looked up and smiled.

"Hello, Victoria," Mr. Reynolds spoke as I took a seat directly across from him.

"Hello, Mr. Reynolds. Please tell me you have some good news for me," I said, jumping to the point.

"In fact, I do," he said, sliding a manila envelope across the table.

I wasted no time emptying its contents and thumbing through all the paperwork. My eyes landed on a photo of a woman who was the spitting image of Ty. They shared the same smooth chocolate skin, they each had a deep dimple on the side of their cheek, and they had the exact same almond-shaped brown eyes. That woman was indeed his mother. Her name was Erica Robinson, and she lived out on Long Island. The paperwork documented her as being a nurse at North Shore Hospital. She was in our reach all this time. I shook my head as I flipped through the rest of the pages.

"The information your mother provided was extremely helpful in terms of helping track her down. What isn't mentioned in the documents is that she isn't married and lives alone with her daughter, who is around thirteen or fourteen years old," Mr. Reynolds said as I stared down at the papers.

"What should I do now?" I asked him, unsure of what my next move should be.

"You must decide if opening this box is worth it. You may uncover things that will change that young man's life for better or worse. You have to be prepared for either before you decide to move forward," Mr. Reynolds stated.

He was absolutely right. Finding Ty's mom would shake his world up. I just hoped it would be for the better. I knew one thing, though: I wasn't going to rush into contacting her. I needed to think the entire thing through before I made a move. When and if the time came, I knew where to find her.

I dug into my wallet and handed Mr. Reynolds an envelope with the remainder of the money he was owed. I thanked him for his services, placed all the documents back into the manila envelope, and left. I needed someone's sound opinion on what to do next, so I headed to Skye's place.

Chapter Twelve

Cameron

"Bro, I need your solid opinion on some shit before we do this," I said to Ty as we sat in the car four houses down from JR's.

"Wassup?" Ty said, looking over at me.

"What you think we should do? I know you ready to ride and just body this nigga, because that's what I want to do, but what is your gut telling you? Should we just let the nigga Harris find the gun and leave it at that or what?" I asked him, expecting his honest, unbiased opinion.

"Wassup with you? You never second-guess yourself," Ty stated. I could tell he was concerned.

"Yeah, but I wanna get shit right with Skye, and I know that's how she wanted to handle it. She and Vic went to great lengths to make sure shit wouldn't fall back on them. I just feel like we should trust them," I stated, looking at the wallpaper on my phone, which was a picture of Skye and Cairo.

Ty didn't say anything back. Instead, he grabbed his nine out of the glove compartment and placed his hand on the door handle. That was all I needed. As long as I had my nigga and he had me, shit would go in our favor.

We hopped out of the car with our weapons concealed and walked in the opposite direction of his house. We weren't trying to risk being seen by anyone going in the front, so we planned to use the back door.

"Remember, Skye said she thought he was wearing a wire. Don't say my name while we are in there, and we gotta put that nigga down before he recognizes one of us and says our names," I told Ty as we crept across his backyard grass.

"I got you," Ty said.

As we stood outside of his back door, we slipped on the ski masks that were in our back pockets. I reached for the doorknob, and of course, it was unlocked. The nigga hadn't learned his lesson about leaving his door unlocked? He was going to learn that day. Back to back, Ty and I entered the house and searched each room on the lower level. There was no JR. We tiptoed up the steps.

We followed the sound of running water that led us outside the bathroom. I looked back at Ty and nodded before kicking the door in. As soon as I had the line on JR, I let off two shots. One pierced his chest, dropping him instantly, and the other was a stray. I walked closer to the shower and pulled the curtain back. I looked down at him as he squirmed and clutched his chest. I watched the water mix with his blood as it flowed down the drain, before raising my gun and emptying the clip in his face.

I admired my handiwork for a second before Ty and I backpedaled out of his crib the same way we entered. When we got back to the car, I told Ty my plan about putting Harris on to the gun that killed Ariana in a few days. The NYPD needed to think I had no idea JR was dead. It was a legit plan, and I was able to sigh, knowing that JR and the threat of someone finding out who was really responsible for what happened to Ariana was nothing but a memory.

I turned on Jay-Z's *Magna Carta Holy Grail* album, and we headed back to Long Island.

Cameron

The shit with JR and the murder weapon worked seamlessly. I hit up Harris a few days after JR's body was discovered and told him one of my niggas put me on and said JR killed Ariana. I told him where he stashed the gun. Harris told me JR was dead, which wasn't news to me, and that he would get on finding the gun. It only took a few hours before he called me back and let me know ballistics were a match to the gun. It was now a closed case.

It was a chill day. Cairo was on Staten Island with his mother, and Vic was visiting them. Ty and I decided to hit the mall. I wanted to cop Skye some shit. She told us she didn't want any gifts or a party, but that wasn't cool with me. Skye deserved the world, and as long as I was alive and breathing, I would provide just that. We still weren't together, but I wasn't trying to pressure her. When she was ready and in the space she wanted to be in, moving forward, she would definitely come back.

"Well, look who it is!" I heard a female voice as Ty and I browsed the women's section of Bloomingdale's.

I turned around toward the direction of the voice, and that's when I saw her. It'd been a minute, but she hadn't changed a bit. She got thicker, but she wore it well. The extra weight complemented her five foot six inch frame well. She had smooth, dark skin, beady brown eyes, and shoulder-length hair, which she always wore with long bangs that almost covered her eyes. She reminded me of a thick Kelly Rowland. She couldn't hold a candle to Skye, but she was still pretty.

"Wassup, Aaliyah?" I finally spoke as she approached Ty and me.

"Hey, stranger. Wassup, Ty?" Aaliyah said, playfully slapping him in the arm and then hugging me.

"It's been forever, shorty. How you been?" I asked, moving her back with my hands on each side of her.

"Yeah, I know, and I'm good. Out here visiting the family for a little bit. I missed you," Aaliyah said, flashing me a gorgeous smile.

I didn't know how to respond to her. The decent thing to do would have been to tell her I missed her too, but I didn't. I hadn't had the chance to miss her. Since I met Skye, she was the only female I thought of constantly outside of my moms and Vic. I didn't wanna hurt Aaliyah's feelings, though, because we had history together. She was my first serious girlfriend back in high school. We met freshman year on the third day of school. She was transferred into my math class. At the time, I was messing with a ton of bitches, but there was something different about Aaliyah. She was quiet and classy, a real step up from the hood chicks who seemed to flock to me.

After spitting a couple lines to her after class, we exchanged numbers. We hit it off instantly and kicked it for the next four years. I still messed with other chicks. I was young and wasn't really tryin'a settle down. Aaliyah was cool with it. She knew she was my main chick and came before the rest. Things with us probably would have progressed, but our relationship ended abruptly when her moms decided to up and move to Ohio.

If it were now, we probably could have made it work, but we were teens who knew nothing about making a long-distance relationship work. My mind was on getting as much pussy as possible, and I couldn't do that if she was in Ohio. So yeah, there was no chance. Seeing her now didn't even make old feelings surface. It just went to show how in love I was with Skye. Thinking about her made me smile.

"What you smiling at, boy? I guess it's safe to say you missed me too," Aaliyah said, snapping me out of my thoughts.

I laughed with her, making her think I was busted when, in actuality, I just wanted to see Skye. "It was nice seeing you, A. We gotta chill before you head back to Ohio," I said, getting my phone out of my pocket so we could exchange numbers.

I handed her the phone, and she handed me hers. After punching in our respective numbers, we switched back. She hugged us, made a promise to call, and walked off with the girl who was accompanying her.

Man

I was scrolling through my phone book, looking for a bitch I could call over and smash when I landed on my cousin's name. I smirked and thought I might as well start putting my plan in motion. After hitting her name, I put the phone to my ear and listened to it ring. I was ready to hang up when she finally answered.

"Wassup, Man," she said into the receiver as she answered.

"What up, cuz? What you doing?" I inquired, even though I wanted to skip the small talk and get to my point. I didn't want her to think I was using her, though.

"At the mall with Mika. Guess who I ran into?" she said, sounding all in love and shit.

"Who?" I asked, not really caring.

"Cameron and Ty. I haven't seen them in so long. They still look the same. Cam still fine as ever. Not that you care about his looks or nothing," Aaliyah replied, chuckling.

Was I that lucky? No wonder she was excited. She and Cam dated back in high school, and I was sure she was still feeling him. Since Aaliyah opened the door mentioning Cam, I took that as my cue to put her on to my plans. At first, she seemed a bit hesitant, but once I explained that they were the ones who killed my brother and Uncle Max and shot me, she was all for it, just like I expected. The good thing about using Aaliyah to help was that she was my blood. Unlike that bitch Ariana, her loyalty would always be to me.

After discussing the plan in detail, we ended up kicking it a little long before deciding to link up later in the week once she had made progress. Once I ended the call with her, I hit up my niggas, letting them know we needed to meet up. Before anything else, I had to put them on game. I needed them to be ready when shit went down, which had to be very soon, seeing as niggas on my end was starting. We had to get back to the paper and fast. A little more patience and everything would fall into place. I was ready!

Chapter Thirteen

Skye

It'd been months since the last incident, and it honestly felt good to have a semi-normal life again. I was looking forward to being back the next semester and everything going well. Everything with JR was behind us, so I was thankful for that. We knew Man was somewhere in the cut waiting to strike, so we were always on alert. I had finally gotten my gun license and had a legal piece that never left my side. I felt safe knowing that I could protect myself and my son if need be.

Cairo was growing so fast right before my eyes, and he found new ways to amaze me every day. I was just getting accustomed to the way things were, but I had an unsettling feeling that trouble was lurking and would soon show its face. I couldn't give too much energy to those thoughts. I focused my energy on doing well in school and being the best mother I could possibly be.

I walked around the Staten Island house that I stayed at with Pop Pop and Hector, doing a little cleaning with Kirk Franklin's "I Smile" playing in the background. It was a Sunday morning ritual that I had picked up since I had been trying to get my life back on track. I wasn't the most religious person and didn't attend church nearly as much as I should have, but I knew and believed in God. Playing gospel on Sunday mornings settled my spirit and made me feel His presence. It worked for me.

"'Today's a new day, but there is no sunshine,'" I sang out as I walked over to get my vibrating phone off the coffee table.

I looked down and saw that it was Cameron calling. I smiled as I answered. We weren't together, but we were in a good place. There was a process, and we were taking the necessary steps to rebuild our foundation. We wanted our next shot to be the last, so we had to do it right.

"Heyyyyyy, sir," I sang out into the phone.

"Wassup, love? What you doing?" he asked before answering his own question. "Oh, never mind. I hear the music," he said, laughing.

I flopped down on the couch and kicked it with him for a little while. I really was happy with the direction we were moving in. We were talking about everything under the sun, laughing, and flirting. Cairo was with him for the weekend, so he had an earful to tell me about what Cai was up to that weekend. There was always something new with Cairo. He possessed the character of one way beyond his months. It was such a joy watching him grow, and hearing about the time he spent with his dad made my heart smile.

Cameron was far from perfect, but he was an amazing dad. I could not have picked a person better suited to be my son's father if I was able to hand pick one myself. He didn't let the bumps in our road affect his relationship with his son, and I really did appreciate that.

"I'll see you tonight, right?" Cameron asked, although I'd already promised to have dinner over his house.

"As promised. I'll be there," I stated, reassuring him.

"A'ight, I love you," he pronounced.

"I love you too," I declared, ending the call.

The remainder of that day went smoothly. I had a chance to do all the things I couldn't do when Cairo was home. He demanded every ounce of my attention. I didn't mind one bit. I loved everything that came along with being his mother. Once my housework was completed and the laundry was put away, I retired to the shower.

After a long day of cleaning and doing laundry, the steamy, hot water that rained down on my body was much needed. Even after washing, I lingered in the shower, just enjoying the feeling until I remembered I had to go to Long Island for dinner. I didn't want to keep them waiting, because I wouldn't hear the end of it. I stepped out of the shower and grabbed my towel off the towel rack before wrapping it around my body.

After entering my bedroom, I dried off and applied Carol's Daughter lotion to my body. I sauntered over to my dresser to retrieve a lace bra and thong set and slipped into them both. In nothing but the bra and thong, I walked over to my closet to look for something to wear. It was just dinner with the family, so I didn't need to get too dressed up. I settled for a pair of jeans and a loose-fitted shirt from Zara. After putting on my clothes, I stepped into a pair of Tory Burch flats. Cute and simple were what I was going for, and I was confident that I succeeded.

I grabbed the Tory Burch bag that matched the flats I was rocking and transferred everything from the bag I wore the previous day into that one before heading out. I was busy singing along to Justin Timberlake's "Mirror" when my phone started ringing. I looked down and scrunched my face because I didn't recognize the number. I didn't hesitate to answer it, though.

"Hello," I answered as I turned down the music.

"Skye, Skye, Skye, how are you?"

Hearing the male voice that was all too familiar sent chills down my spine. "Miguel," I said dryly, contemplating hanging up.

"Don't sound too excited to hear from me. I told you I'd be in touch. I'm glad you got your son back and that everything is well with Cameron," Miguel said, letting out a low chuckle.

It bothered me so much that Miguel seemed to always have one up. He knew all of the moves probably before they were even made.

"What is it that you want from me?" I asked, hoping he would get to the point.

"To pick up where I left off with Cameron," he said matter-of-factly.

"That's not going to happen," I stated.

"I think you're a smart girl, so you know that answer will not suffice," Miguel retorted, raising his voice.

"Well, that's the fucking answer you will be getting. Don't call me anymore with your bullshit. You asked for the money, you got the money, now please leave me the hell alone," I shouted before ending the call.

I wasn't going to let Miguel ruin the mood I'd found myself in earlier. I was going to have dinner with my extended family, and all thoughts of him needed to be pushed to the back of my mind.

I was happy that Victoria had decided to go home with me. It was nice having her to hang out with. Living on Staten Island, I'd had more lonely nights than I had become accustomed to. I had Cairo, but there wasn't much he and I could do. It wasn't like we could hold a conversation about how our day was. Nonetheless, I loved every minute of being a mom. Pop Pop and Hector were always on the go, so they were no use in terms of keeping me company either.

It was a few weeks later when we strolled through the Americana mall. Cairo was laid back in his stroller, enjoying being chauffeured around, and Victoria was right beside me.

"We about to swipe the strip off the back of my brother's card," Victoria said, making a credit card swipe gesture with her hands.

I laughed at her, partially because only she would say something like that and partially because it was true. Even though Cameron and I weren't together, he made sure Cairo and I were good in every aspect. He knew that I had plenty of cash and never needed a dime from him, but that didn't stop him from being a provider. Anything I purchased with Cameron's money was always for our son. Cairo was his responsibility, not me, so I didn't deem it necessary to spend his cash on myself.

Our first stop was the food court. Being pregnant, Victoria felt the urge to eat everything her eyes landed on. I couldn't complain, because I was the same way when I was pregnant with Cairo.

"What you trying to eat?" I asked her as we browsed the variety of food options.

"I'm straight with a pretzel for right now," she responded, pointing over where Auntie Anne's Pretzels was located.

I was happy with her choice. It wasn't an official mall trip unless an Auntie Anne's pretzel was involved. We headed over to the booth and waited in line until it was our turn. I ordered two plain pretzels for Victoria and me, but I made sure hers was unsalted. I definitely wasn't trying to have her pressure shoot through the roof during her pregnancy. I knew Cairo would want to eat my pretzel, so I ordered him unsalted pretzel bites, something he could munch on while we shopped.

After paying for our pretzels, we were on our way outside to the strip where the stores were located. Americana wasn't like the normal mall where you went inside a building to find a bunch of different stores. The stores there were located outside, similar to the setup of an outlet.

As soon as we stepped out into the August heat, I spotted the Ralph Lauren store. That had to be our first stop. My son wore so much Ralph Lauren you would think he was a baby model for them. I considered it.

Once inside the Ralph Lauren store, I picked up everything I laid my eyes on that Cairo didn't have yet. There were just so many cute things for little boys, and my son deserved to have it all. As long as Cameron and I were able, that's how it would always be for Cairo. We even picked up a ton of things for Victoria's baby. They were neutral things like onesies since we didn't know the sex yet. By the time I relieved Ralph Lauren of most of their baby stock, I had a tab of over $1,500.

"Cairo is too damn spoiled," Victoria said as we made our way to the next store.

I heard her, but I sort of tuned her out as I zoomed my focus on a Spanish guy I'd spotted near Auntie Anne's. It could have been a coincidence that he too liked Ralph Lauren, but to be safe, I dug into my Chanel bag to make sure my Nina was tucked away in case she was needed.

"It's y'all fault, too. Everybody says I spoil this little boy. Your baby next," I retorted, still eyeing the Spanish man suspiciously.

Victoria and I laughed as we went in and out of a few of our favorite stores. We stopped by Tiffany & Co., where I purchased my mother and Mariah earrings just so they knew that I appreciated them. We were walking out of the Juicy Couture store when I spotted the Spanish man again. There weren't that many coincidences in the world. I didn't want to make Victoria panic, so I made up an excuse to leave.

"Girl, let's head home. We can hit the rest of these stores when we don't have Cairo. I don't want my baby to catch sunburn." I laughed nervously, hoping she didn't catch wind that I was indeed panicking my-damn-self. If it had been just Victoria and me, I would have been fine. Having my son with us made shit a lot riskier.

"I saw him. I didn't want you to panic," Victoria revealed to me.

I should have known she wasn't oblivious that we were being followed. I didn't respond to her. I just smiled and focused on making it back to my truck. Once we were at the car, I wasted no time strapping Cairo into his car seat and double-checking that he was secure. I didn't know what was going to happen, but I knew that I would die protecting my son. Acting as if everything were normal, Victoria and I climbed in the driver and passenger seats of the truck and were ready to roll.

As I maneuvered through the parking lot, I instructed Victoria to get my gun out of my purse in case we needed to use it. I would rather she be ready versus fidgeting to get the gun in the heat of the moment. Just as I stopped at the red light that separated the parking lot from ongoing traffic, a black Tahoe slammed into my side of the truck. I yelped out in pain and slammed my foot on the gas, sending my truck flying into traffic.

"What the fuck!" Victoria screamed out just as the bullets began to beat into my truck.

My entire left side was on fire from the impact of being hit, but I had to get to my son. I sped through traffic as our assailants trailed us, letting loose their weapons. I swerved on the highway, barely missing the Camry that had the right of way. I glanced back at Cairo, who was releasing a piercing scream.

"Mommy is here, Cairo," I said, trying to soothe him with the tone of my voice.

My hands were trembling as I tried to maintain control of the wheel. The gunfire didn't cease. I turned my head just as a bullet went flying through my window, missing my head by inches.

"Victoria, I don't know how we going to do this, but I need you to get control of the wheel. I gotta get Cairo," I screamed over the sound of guns blazing.

If it weren't for my impeccable driving skills, we all would have looked like Swiss cheese. I screamed at Victoria to snap out her trance and to get her to listen to my instructions. I waited for her to grip the wheel before I attempted to climb into the back seat.

I heard the back window shatter and felt a burning sensation in my back. I knew I had been shot as the pain intensified. I couldn't stop, though. I fumbled with the buckles on Cairo's car seat and was hit again. I cried out in pain, but I would fight to my last breath to protect my son. Freeing Cairo from his car seat, I picked him up and laid him on the floor between the front and back seats. By that time, I was hunched over him, going in and out of consciousness.

I heard Victoria calling out my name, and I thought I was responding. I felt my lips move, but there was no sound. The pain I was in was overpowering every last one of my senses. Cairo cried and squirmed beneath me, so I knew he was okay. I was in the middle of praying when the truck jerked, and everything went black.

Victoria

I struggled to open my eyes. They were heavy and felt superglued shut. I fought to remember what happened until the beeping sound coming from the machines alerted me that I was in the hospital. Flashes of the incident came back to me at once, causing me to panic. Was I shot? Where were Skye and Cairo? Was my baby okay? I fought a little harder before my eyelids finally let me take over and fluttered open.

I attempted to move my head left then right, but the excruciating pain in my head stopped me. I felt around the side of me for the button that I knew would be present. There was always a button for patients to hit when they needed a nurse or their doctor. Once my fingers ran across it, I used what strength I had and pressed the button. Moments later, a short, chubby lady who looked to be of Indian descent came walking into my room.

"Look who is awake," she said, flashing me a warm smile.

I attempted to speak, and she stopped me, grabbing the pitcher off the table beside my bed. She poured some water into a cup and came closer to me.

"Take slow and steady sips," she instructed as she held the cup to my lips. "I'm Nurse Singh. Do you know where you are?" she asked, setting the cup back down on the table.

I nodded. She proceeded to ask me if I remembered how I landed in the hospital, and I nodded again.

"Good. I'm going to step out and return with your doctor." She turned to walk away, and I grabbed her arm. It wasn't rough, but it had enough force to stop her in her tracks. She turned back around toward me.

"My baby?" I asked with tears welling up.

She pointed to one of the screens, which had wires that were pasted on my stomach. "This machine monitors the heartrate of the baby. At first, we were worried because the baby was indeed in distress, but once we stabilized your pressure, the baby's heartrate stabilized as well. He or she is doing fine, I assure you. Please let me get your doctor so he can fill you in on everything else." She smiled and sauntered out of the room.

I prayed that Cairo and Skye were okay as I lay back with my eyes closed.

"Hello." The male voice brought me out of my thoughts.

"Hi," I said weakly as I struggled to sit up.

He approached my side and helped me.

Cameron

I looked over at Aaliyah, and she was snoozing. I laughed, because I'd told her that this wack-ass movie was going to have one of us knocked out. I grabbed one of the pillows that I was leaning on and slid it underneath her head. She moved a little but didn't wake up. I stood from the seat I was occupying on the couch and walked into the kitchen, where I found Ty stuffing his face.

"Nigga, you sure Vic pregnant and not you?" We shared a laughed.

He couldn't debate with what I said because he knew he ate a lot. If it weren't for our workout sessions and impromptu ball games, my nigga would be on his Rick Ross shit.

"You and Liyah was looking pretty cozy, my nigga," Ty spoke between the sips he took from his water.

"Nah, it's not even like that. She cool, but she already know what it is with me and Skye. She don't even try to overstep," I said, opening the fridge and grabbing a bottle of water.

"For now," Ty said nonchalantly.

I sat down across from him and opened my water. I knew Ty wasn't feeling Aaliyah, but what he said made me think. The conversation about me and Skye came up a lot during the time I been kicking it with Aaliyah. I made it very clear each time that I had every intention of being with Skye. If Aaliyah didn't take me seriously, she would only end up being hurt in the end. I was never one to string chicks along, so I kept it one hundred out of the gate. We were cool, and I wanted to keep it on a friendship level. The minute I felt like she was trying to overstep that, she was getting cut the fuck off.

The vibration of my cell phone brought me out of my thoughts. I dug down into the pockets of my cargos and got it. I glanced at the number and thought about ignoring it because it wasn't a contact already saved in my phone. I went against that and slid my finger across the screen before pressing it to my ear.

"What up," I spoke into the phone.

"Hello, is this Cameron Carter?" a female voice spoke.

"Yeah, who is this?" I asked.

"Hello, Mr. Carter. I am Nurse Singh from North Shore University Hospital. We have two patients here by the names of Victoria Carter and Skye Lewis. Your name was given as a contact. Are you of any relation to them?" she asked.

All I heard were Vic's and Skye's names. Everything else was blocked out.

"Are they okay? I'm on my way," I declared, signaling for Ty to follow me.

"I can't give any details of their conditions over the phone, but I will gladly assist you once you get here," she declared.

I thanked her before walking in the living room and waking up Aaliyah. I apologized for interrupting her sleep and explained it was an emergency. We all left the house together and hopped in my truck. I thought, *I can't show up to the hospital with Aaliyah.* Skye knew I was kicking it with her, but still, I would never disrespect her in that manner. Aaliyah was never around when Skye or Cairo was present.

"Liyah, my sister and my shorty in the hospital. I mean, Skye," I started to explain.

"I hope everything is okay, Cam. I'll call a cab. It's not a problem. Just text me and let me know they both are well when you can. Later, Ty," she said before climbing out of the back seat.

I appreciated that she wasn't one of those chicks who just loved drama. She understood her position in my life. I never treated her like she was nothing, because we did have history, but I didn't treat her like she came before Skye. That would never happen.

Once she was away from the car, I started it up, and Ty and I were on the way to North Shore. I explained to him what the nurse told me while he texted my moms and Adriana. Pop Pop and Hector were in town, so I had him text them as well and tell them to meet us at the hospital.

I'd barely parked when I jumped out of the car and ran into the emergency room. I didn't know what to think, especially because Cairo was with them and his name was never mentioned. I spoke briefly to the receptionist before Ty and I were escorted by security to the trauma unit. I spoke briefly to the nurse at the nurse's station, who happened to be Nurse Singh, the one who had made the call. She was nice, but I didn't have time for pleasantries.

"There was a child with them," I uttered to her as she led Ty and me to Vic's room.

By that time, we were there at Vic's room, and I heard Cairo as I stepped into the room. He was sitting on some woman's lap, and Vic was looking directly at him with tears in her eyes. I automatically picked up Cairo, not caring that the woman protested.

"This is my son," I shouted as I walked over to Vic's bed and stood beside Ty.

"Skye needs you, Cam," she said before gesturing for me to give Cairo to Ty.

I did just that and backpedaled out of the room in search of the nurse who had shown me to Vic's room. When I found her, I asked if she could take me to Skye, and she kindly obliged. I walked into Skye's room and felt as if my world was spinning out of control. There were two doctors standing beside her bed, and as I got closer, I saw that she was lying on her stomach and her leg was in a cast.

"Are you a relative?" one of the doctors asked, briefly taking his attention off of Skye.

"I . . . I'm Cameron. Her . . ." I stuttered to get my sentence out. I was relieved when he began speaking over me.

"She has been asking for you," he said, stepping back from Skye and giving me space to be by her side.

I put my hand in hers, and she squeezed it.

"How is she?" I asked, looking at the doctor for answers.

He took a deep breath before giving me a breakdown of Skye's condition. She had been shot twice in her back. One bullet was through and through, while they had to perform surgery to remove the other. She had a broken leg and a fractured rib. *What the fuck happened?* I thought, trying to mask the emotional breakdown I was on the verge of having. I thought I heard all there was to hear when the doctor who was closest to me put his hand on my shoulder.

"The baby is fine right now, but we are not sure that it will go full term. Ms. Lewis went through a lot of trauma, and the baby may be affected," he uttered in a sincere manner.

I felt the hold she had on my hand tighten, and I knew that she was hurting ten times worse than I was. I had no idea that she was pregnant, but I knew for a fact it was my baby. We weren't together, but I hit it on a regular basis, and Skye wasn't fucking with anyone else. That shit hurt me to the core. Just the thought of our baby not making it was a hard pill to swallow. If the baby could just hang in there, I made a silent promise to him or her that I would do everything possible to make the rest of Skye's pregnancy stress free. I couldn't wait to get the full story and bury whoever the fuck was behind this shit.

The doctors excused themselves and left me alone with Skye, which I was thankful for. We needed the time alone. Even if we spent it in silence, we needed it.

I tried to let go of her hand, and she tightened the hold she had on mine.

"I'm not leaving you, shorty. I just wanna grab the chair so I can sit next to you. I promise I'm not going to leave you, Skye," I reassured her.

She slowly let go of the grasp she had on my hand, and I walked a few feet away and grabbed a chair. Placing it directly beside her bed, I took a seat and put my hand in hers once more. I stared at her and watched the tears streaming down her cheeks. I couldn't suppress mine any longer, so I cried with her.

"I'm sorry," was all I could say.

She tried to speak. "Cai . . ."

I leaned closer so that I could hear her clearly. Her voice was low and raspy, but I knew she was asking about Cairo.

"He's okay, baby. He's perfectly fine. Ty has him. Want me to get him?" I spoke.

She nodded and let go of my hand, signaling that it was okay for me to leave for the moment. I quickly maneuvered through the hospital until I got to Victoria's room. I saw that she was smiling, so I knew she was okay. Plus, Ty was there, so I didn't need to linger around. I grabbed Cairo and headed back to Skye's room. When we walked in, she was knocked out. I was kind of glad because I knew as long as she was up, she was in pain. At least she could relax for a bit, even if her sleep was short-lived.

Skye

I woke up in severe pain. I tried to move, but my attempts were futile. I took a few breaths to get the pain under control and fluttered my eyes open. The first thing I laid eyes on made me smile. Cameron was sitting right beside my bed with Cairo in his arms. Cairo was knocked out. Cameron had his eyes closed, but I knew he wasn't asleep. There were voices coming from behind me, but I couldn't bear the pain of turning my head to see who was there. I knew one voice was my mother's. She spoke above everyone else.

"Cameron," I whispered, gently squeezing his hand.

His eyes shot open, and he leaned forward with the vein bulging out his forehead. "She's up," he announced. "Are you okay?" he said, returning his attention to me.

I nodded and closed my eyes for a second. "Thank you, God," I said before opening my eyes again. I had to thank Him because I was looking at His gift to me, and he was safe and unharmed. I would get shot all over if it meant protecting my son.

"Skye, I need to know about the gun they found at the scene. Please tell me it's the one we got registered," my mother said as she walked from behind me and stood next to Cameron.

I thought about the gun and sighed in relief because it was indeed the gun Cameron had insisted that I register, and it was clean. I gave her a half smile and nodded.

"Thank God, baby girl. I just couldn't deal with this on top of a gun charge," she said, bending over and kissing me on the cheek. As she stood up straight, she continued to talk. "I know you are not up for it, but we need to know what happened."

She was right. I didn't want to talk about it, so I ignored her and motioned for Cameron to come closer.

"Yes, baby, what you need?" he questioned.

"Can you please get the nurse? I want to turn over and hold Cairo," I said.

He nodded before standing up and handing Cairo to my mother. His seat was taken by my dad. If I could move, I would have jumped right into his arms. I was so happy to see him. Lately, he had been burying himself in work to the point where he had to be gone weeks at a time. I didn't understand and wanted answers, but in that moment, I was just happy to see his face.

"Hi, princess," he said, moving a loose strand of hair out of my face.

"Daddy, I'm so happy to see you," I whispered.

"Rest, Skye. I'm not going anywhere," he stated.

"Harvey, she needs to tell us what happened," my mother voiced.

"Not right now, Adriana," my father asserted.

He shot her a look of contempt, and I saw defeat in her eyes. I had never seen that type of interaction between the two of them, and I wanted to know what the problem was. Maybe Dad found out the secrets Mom had been keeping. That would have surely rubbed him the wrong way. I didn't know, though. I just didn't see my mother indulging in that information with him, and I knew for sure Pop Pop wouldn't.

"Dad, what's going on?" I inquired.

He looked up at my mother and frowned. "You care to share with our daughter why I'm pissed off, or should I?" he said, turning his head back to me.

My mother went to talk but was cut off by the voice I recognized to be Hector's. "Not here, Harvey," Hector said, stepping closer to my mother.

"If I wanted your opinion, I would have asked you for it. Why the fuck you here anyway?" my father spoke as he stood from his seat.

Hector went to respond but was interrupted by the nurse, asking them to clear the room so she could clean my bandages and help me turn over.

It took her a little over twenty minutes to clean me up and help me turn over on my back. Leaning back on the wounds that were surgically stitched closed hurt like hell. I had to deal with it because I wanted to hold my son in my arms. Having him so close and not being able to touch him was hurting.

When my family returned, Cairo was wide awake, so I was happy. I was saddened to see that my father was no longer there, and neither was Pop Pop. I asked about their disappearance, and my mom told me that Pop Pop went to talk to my father outside and that they both would be back. That made me feel a bit better. Cameron placed Cairo in my arms, and I winced in pain. My rib was on fire, but I was dead set on pushing through the pain to hold my son.

"Mommy is so happy that you are okay, Cai," I whispered to Cairo before kissing him on his forehead.

Cameron had returned to his seat and laid his head on the edge of my bed. I reached down and massaged his head. He was stressing over the condition I was in, on top of the news that our baby may or may not make it full term. I couldn't help but think that if I had never turned down Miguel's proposition, this would have never happened.

Pop Pop

I knew why Harvey was frustrated. I understood completely. However, he needed to get a hold of his emotions and deal with the situation at a later time. Skye was in no position to deal with her parents' drama, and neither was I. Everyone made the decisions they made, and now we all had to deal with them. Harvey included.

"*Nieta,* are you ready to tell us what happened?" I asked, walking back into Skye's room and moving closer to the bed.

"Not really, but I know that I have to," Skye said, handing Cairo back to Cameron and sitting back.

As she sat back on the bed, she winced in pain. I was ready to murder whoever put her in this situation. I took a lot of things lightly, but messing with my family, money, or livelihood was not one of those things.

"The sooner we know the details, the quicker we can handle it," I said, gently rubbing her hand.

I stared intently at Skye and noticed that she was in contemplation, or maybe she was trying to prepare what she would say in her head. I wasn't going to rush her, but I was growing impatient. While I was outside speaking to Harvey, I'd made a phone call back home. Reinforcements would be arriving soon, and by that time, I wanted to have enough information for them to get the job done and head back to Panama.

"A few weeks ago, I got a call from Miguel," Skye started to explain.

"Why wouldn't you tell me?" Cameron said with a look of contempt written across his once-neutral expression.

"I didn't want you getting worked up or back into beef with him over something I could handle. At least, I thought I could handle it. He told me he wanted me to get your organization back in business with him. I didn't even need to think about it. My answer was no off the bat. He made a few threats, and I hung up on him. That was the end of that. Today Vic, Cairo, and I were at Americana, shopping, and I spotted a Spanish dude following us. I knew it had to be Miguel's people because we not beefing with any other Spanish team. I just wanted to get Cairo to safety, that's all. I knew Vic and I could handle ourselves. It happened so fast, like a scene from *Bad Boys II*. We were in the car, headed out of the parking lot, and a truck slammed into mine. Although my side was on fire, I knew I couldn't stop. That's when the gunfire started. We had to think fast. I let Victoria get control of the wheel while I climbed in the back to shield Cairo. That's when I got shot." Skye paused, swallowing the lump that formed in her throat.

She struggled to keep her tears at bay but inevitably lost the battle. "If I didn't climb back there, Cairo would have been shot," she cried.

I pulled her close to me gently and rubbed the back of her head while she cried in my chest. "It's okay, *nieta*. Cairo is fine. You saved him. You protected him like a mother should," I said in an attempt to console her.

I looked over at Cameron, who hadn't said a word, and saw that he was on the verge of exploding. I knew it was because of two things: one, his girl and son were put in harm's way, and two, it was his beef that caused it.

"Miguel?" Adriana questioned after picking her brain, trying to figure out where she knew the name from.

It was what I feared. Unbeknownst to any of them, Adriana and Miguel had history.

"Not now," I uttered, shooting her a glare that told her to keep her mouth shut.

"That motherfucker is dead!" Adriana shouted, disregarding what I told her.

Skye watched the scene unfold and was completely confused. Her mother's outburst would surely open Pandora's box. Skye would have questions no one was prepared to answer.

"I should have killed that motherfucker, too! I just knew I should have!" Adriana screamed as she paced the floor.

I shook my head, knowing it was time to put all the cards on the table. The secrets we held in the dark could no longer be kept as they were forcing their own way out into the light.

Skye

Watching my mother's reaction to finding out this was Miguel's doing really confused me. How in the world did she know Miguel? Even if the name was familiar, how did she automatically know it was the Miguel she knew? What did she mean by "kill him, too"? I wanted answers, but something nagging at me told me I wouldn't like, nor would I be able to handle the answers. Thinking about it made me look around the room again. My father had never returned, and that saddened me.

"What's going on here?" I asked, looking at Pop Pop for answers.

He sighed and looked as if he was ready to speak, but the words didn't come out. I looked from Pop Pop to my mother then over to Hector. Even he looked as if someone killed his puppy. The tension in the room was so thick it could have been cut with a knife.

"Mom," I called out weakly.

The medicine was starting to take effect again, but I fought it as I began to get drowsy. I wasn't going to sleep until I got answers.

"What exactly do you want to know, Skye?" my mother said, sounding as if she really didn't want to indulge in the conversation.

"Everything," I stated.

She came closer to my bed and grabbed my hand. I mentally prepared myself for what she was going to say. It had to be serious just by the way they were all acting. She had my undivided attention, and Cameron's as well.

There was no way I could have expected or been prepared for what my mother revealed to me. She started off explaining that she had, in fact, been in contact with Pop Pop even though her mother did not know. My mother explained that once she went away to school, she was free to contact him without the worry of her mother finding out. However, it wasn't the first time. Every summer while she was in high school, she was in Panama, and her mother thought she was spending it with her aunt. Pop Pop's sister, Yasmine, lived in Florida and stayed in touch with my grandmother even after she and Pop Pop split. Yasmine thought my mom deserved to be in her father's life, so she didn't mind lying to my mother and sending my mom to Panama when she was supposed to be in Florida with her.

During the time she spent with Pop Pop, the allure of the life he lived called her. It started with her doing minor things like keeping books, sitting in on meetings, and meeting new clients, but it quickly escalated. During her sophomore year of high school, her brother, my uncle, was murdered. Colon, Panama is a pretty small place, and in addition to that, everyone knew and respected Pop Pop. It didn't take long for him to get the names of those behind the hit. It was Los Jefes, which at that time was run by Miguel's father. Of course, my grandfather returned to Panama with murder on his mind, but not too far behind was my mother. She expressed that she had to be one the one to avenge her brother's death, because although they lived apart, he was everything to her. Pop Pop didn't like the idea, but he knew in his heart that my mother could pull it off, so he allowed it.

After weeks of planning her next move, she was ready. She boarded a flight to Mexico with one thing on her mind: blood. Miguel's father, Ricardo, was hard to get to, but she didn't mind killing a few of his minions off to get to him. She knew having patience would pay off, and it did in the best way. After killing Ricardo, my mother said she returned home as if nothing happened, finished high school, and was off to Howard. While attending school at Howard, my mother ended up becoming a supplier to the DMV area. She could have expanded but didn't want to stray too far from her studies, which were still her main priority. She continued to visit my Pop Pop, but they never spoke of the Ricardo–Los Jefes situation again.

I looked at her, confused. My mother, Ms. Goody Two-Shoes, was a murderer and a drug dealer. I just couldn't wrap my head around that. She'd scolded me for the exact same things she had done. I couldn't even bear to look at her. I felt like the woman who gave birth to me was a stranger. I didn't know who she was. The day I was lying in the hospital bed with gunshot wounds and a broken leg was the day my mother decided to introduce herself to me. I didn't want to hear any more, but she continued.

"That's when Hector . . ." she said before being cut off by my father, who had now returned to the room.

"Don't you fucking dare," my father said while giving my mother a look that could have dropped her where she stood.

"She told her everything. She might as well put it all on the table," Hector said, once again jumping to my mother's defense.

"He's right," my mother uttered before turning her attention back to me. She picked up where she left off as my father stood in the corner, shaking his head.

"I met Hector during the summers I visited," she said.

I didn't know where she was headed, but I knew it wasn't anywhere good. "Mom, please stop. I don't want to know any more. Please," I begged, hoping she would take heed and drop the subject altogether.

Surprisingly, she did. She stepped back away from my bed and stood beside my father, who moved over, putting a little distance between them. He thought I didn't notice it, but I did. After the revelations she made, I didn't have the energy to question anything else. I was ready for them all to go except Cameron. Just as I was going to speak up and let them know I didn't want the company anymore, Hector moved closer, standing in the spot my mother previously stood. He looked down at me and smiled. I had never paid attention to his facial expressions or his features before because it wasn't necessary. However, in that moment, I already knew. There was something familiar about him that reached beyond the months we had spent around each other.

"Skye, I'm your father," Hector declared, putting an end to all the speculation I had.

It felt like I had been stabbed in the chest repeatedly. I fought to catch my breath as I slowly slipped into hyperventilation. Hector reached down in an attempt to calm me down, but I quickly pushed his hands away. I didn't want him to touch me. They were liars! Each and every one of them lied to me in some way. I could have dealt with my mother having a secret life on the side, but Hector being my dad was something I really couldn't wrap my head around. It's like my entire life as I knew it was one big-ass cover-up. I wasn't sure about anything at the point. Except for Cairo and Cameron. Cairo wasn't old enough to lie to me, and Cameron, although he had been a jerk, never was disloyal to me.

I looked over to him, and he had the same expression-less face I had. He moved closer to me as if to protect me, and he began to read my thoughts. No, I wasn't psychic, nor did Cameron and I share some sort of telepathic ability, but he knew what I was thinking. We were connected like that. He nodded to let me know he got me and stood from his seat.

"A'ight, y'all, it's a lot for her to take in right now. So I'm saying, everyone just dip and let her rest. Cairo and I will stay, and if anything changes, I'll definitely call," Cameron said in a serious tone.

They all looked over at me as if I was going to object, but I wasn't. He spoke exactly what I was feeling. They needed to be gone yesterday. Noticing that I wasn't going to go against what Cameron said, they each gave me an empty apology and left me alone with my boys.

Chapter Fourteen

Victoria

I lay in bed, thanking God over and over for sparing all of our lives. Especially my baby and Cairo. They were innocent and didn't deserve to pay for the mistakes we made. I put my hand on top of Ty's, which was resting on my protruding belly.

"Fuck!" I cried out as a sharp pain shot through my stomach.

"Babe, you good?" Ty asked, jumping up from his seat.

"I think something is wrong," I cried out as the pain hit me again. This time it was followed by a gush of water, which flowed freely onto the bed beneath me. "No, not my baby," I cried while Ty got up to get a nurse.

Between the pain and the beeping of the machines, I couldn't focus. All that played over and over was the nurse yelling out that I was in labor. I was only six months pregnant. It wasn't time. The baby was not ready. I couldn't comprehend why this was happening to me. Moments ago, they had said everything was fine.

Ty held on to my hand until we reached the entrance of the operating room. He was stopped by the surgeon and denied access. I wished they would have allowed him to be in the room with me, but I couldn't think about that too long. I needed to talk to God while I still had a chance. If it was anyone's time to go, I prayed it was mine. *Please spare my baby,* was what I kept repeating to God before I blacked out.

I woke up inside a hospital room, cold and alone. A single tear escaped my eye as I tried to understand why Ty or my mother wasn't present with me. I felt my stomach. It was protruding, but not like it was prior to me blacking out. *Did my baby die?* I thought, fighting back tears. I felt around at my side before finding the button I was looking for. Moments later, a nurse appeared at my side. I stared at her through squinted eyes. I was convinced in that moment that I was dreaming. It all had to be a nightmare.

"Ms. Carter, I'm glad you are awake," the nurse said, smiling, showing me the deep dimples that were strategically placed on each side of her cheek.

"Where am I?" I asked. I needed to know that this was all real.

"North Shore University Hospital," the nurse said, giving me a concerned look.

It was real. I was indeed here alone, without my baby, and she was indeed Ty's mother.

"My baby?" I asked, frightened by the answer she would give me.

"He's in the NICU. Your mother and boyfriend are there with him. He's in good hands, Ms. Carter. Your doctor will be in shortly to give you official details of his status," she explained.

I sighed a bit of relief. I was aware that being born three months early put my baby at a lot of risk, but he was alive. Wow, we had a boy. Ty and I wanted to be surprised about the sex, but I was ecstatic finding out that we gave birth to a baby boy. Knowing that he was alive and Ty and my mother were with him really did put me at ease. There was another concern, though. The more she spoke, her mannerisms that Ty clearly inherited from her started to show. This was her. There was no doubt in my mind. I remembered her face from the picture. There's no way I could forget it.

"Excuse me," I said, giving her a confused expression.

"Yes, what's wrong?" the nurse turned to me and asked.

I wanted to know. Ty deserved to know. Maybe it wasn't the right time.

"Oh, never mind, everything is fine," I stated, concluding that we'd deal with it at another time.

"Okay, sweetie, I will be back to check on you in a bit," the nurse spoke, turning to leave.

I couldn't just let her go. It was now or never.

"Erica?" I called out her name, instantly getting her attention.

She looked at me through slanted eyes and gave me a half smile. "Does he know, Victoria?" she asked, moving closer to my bed.

How did she know I knew? I shook my head no and saw her facial expression go from tense to relaxed.

"He can't know. I'm supposed to be out of the country. I couldn't leave my baby boy behind, although Jeff threatened to kill me if I didn't. I've looked after him from a distance his entire life. It killed me that I couldn't reach out to him, but things were better with me out of the picture," she started to explain.

"Jeff is dead," I said, not allowing her to finish. If Jeff was who was keeping her away from Ty all these years, she no longer had that barrier in place. She was about to begin speaking when Ty walked into the room.

Ty began speaking as soon as he got near my bed. "Baby, I'm so glad you're up. You should see him. We had a son. My little man. He's so tiny, but he going to be a'ight."

I held his hand and listened to him share the experience of seeing our son for the first time. He was unable to hold him but was able to touch his hands and feet through the holes in the incubator, and that was good with him. Our son, who he kept calling TJ while he spoke, was alive, and that's all that mattered. Whatever needed to be done in terms of his health would just be done. Erica stood back, giving Ty and me space with a smile plastered on her face. She looked proud, and I knew she was. Her only son had just become a dad.

I listened to Ty talk about TJ and our future plans as a family until the medicine took over, and I drifted off to sleep.

Skye

Cameron and I sat in silence while Cairo slept. I was glad he didn't want to talk at that moment. He understood that I was trying to understand it all. I was sure he was too. I was struggling to wrap my head around what was revealed to me. It was too much, and Pop Pop was right. It wasn't the time, nor was it the appropriate venue for them to drop those bombs on me. It just wasn't fair. I was lied to my entire life. What made matters worse was that they each had ample time to be honest. There was always an opportunity. Pop Pop should have told me about my mother and Miguel the minute he found out.

I couldn't believe my mother. I knew there was something she was keeping from me from the reaction she gave when she saw Hector. That was her chance. She could have pulled me to the side and explained everything to me. Or when she was busy yelling and trying to scold me for taking over for Cameron. She could have said she was speaking from experience, but no, she chose to lie. They all did.

My room door opened, and my father, Harvey, poked his head in. I didn't want to talk to him either. It was evident in my facial expression, but that didn't stop him from coming in. Before I knew it, he was standing beside my bed staring at me.

"Princess, I know that you don't want to be bothered right now, but I need for you to hear me out," he stated.

I said nothing. I turned my head toward Cameron, who took it upon himself to take Cairo from me and exit the room, leaving me, Harvey, and thick tension.

"Skye, look at me, please," my father spoke.

The hurt in his voice forced me to turn my head and look at him.

Once he was satisfied that he had my attention, he started to explain himself again. Although I didn't want to listen, I did. My father revealed to me that when my mother found out she was pregnant, she was honest and told him that she had slept with Hector during a visit to Panama. He knew there was a possibility I wasn't his from the beginning, but that didn't stop him from loving my mother or the child growing inside of her.

When I was born, he and my mother flew out to Panama to talk with Hector, who had no idea that my mother was pregnant. He was shocked but was willing to do what was in my best interest. He knew that there was no way he could just up and leave Panama and fly to the States to raise me, and there was no way my mother was going to leave me there with him and Pop Pop. They came to the conclusion that it was best that my mother and Harvey stayed together and raised me. They all agreed not to get a DNA test because it made no sense. Harvey was my dad, and that was it. It didn't stop Hector from sending money or presents to the States for me. My father wasn't bothered by that at all. They had mutual respect for each other until he found out that my mother got a paternity test done on me and Hector behind his back. Although he was pissed, he still didn't get angry. He accepted the results for what they were and continued to raise me. That was the plan. He wasn't straying from it.

My dad expressed that finding out that Hector was in New York and thoroughly involved in my life was what pushed him to bury himself in work. Dealing with the possibility that I would find out that Hector was my dad and allow him to come between us was too painful for my father. I understood that completely, but what I didn't understand was how he could think that.

"You think that's all it takes for someone to replace you in my life, Dad?" I asked. He looked at me without saying a word, so I continued. "Nothing or no one can replace you. You are the only father I know and have known my entire life. That can't be eradicated. You have been here for me in the worst of times. You have loved me unconditionally. Hector and I have been getting to know each other, and I have grown to love him for what he has done for me lately. It still doesn't compare to the love I have for you. I'm not upset about the situation. Things happen. I respect you for standing up and taking care of me without complaints, even though you were aware that I wasn't your biological daughter. What hurts me is that you guys lied. You all didn't trust me enough with that truth, and that really hurts, Dad," I spoke in a whisper.

"I'm sorry for the secrets, I'm sorry for the lies, and most of all I'm sorry for hurting you, Skye. You are my world. I can't lose you," my dad said, leaning down and kissing my forehead.

"You won't," I declared.

I didn't want to talk about it anymore, so I asked him to go and get Cameron and Cairo. He was a little hesitant at first, but eventually, he did what I asked.

Chapter Fifteen

Pop Pop

I felt really bad leaving the hospital and leaving Skye to deal with our revelations on her own, but I needed to set things in motion. I knew this day would come the moment I found out who Cameron was working for, but I wanted to prolong it until Skye was out of harm's way, which was why I convinced her to pay him the money. If she hadn't been pregnant at the time, things would have gone totally differently. There was no use reflecting on how things would have been different. It was time to move forward in rectifying the situation.

My plans had to be changed. I had my men change their route and head to Mexico instead of coming to the States. Hector and I were going to be arriving shortly after. Since Miguel was roaming the streets of the United States, his home would be under less protection than it would be if he were indeed there. There would be guards, but nothing that my men couldn't handle. Adriana insisted on going to Mexico with us, but I needed her to tie up the loose ends in the States when the time presented itself. It took us the entire ride to the airport for me to convince her that I knew what I was doing, and my plan was foolproof. Hector and I promised to be in touch before boarding the plane for Mexico.

When we arrived, we were greeted by three of my men who would escort us to the safe house I had there.

I made it my business to have property in every place I would potentially end up for the exact reason I was there. Miguel wasn't one who stayed idle for too long, so we had to move at twice his speed. There was no time to waste. Every single minute wasted pushed us further away from being able to successfully complete the mission.

When we reached the safe house, my men were there and ready to fill me in on all the information they had gathered while staking out Miguel's estate and waiting for our arrival. Just as I expected, there was a small army of men guarding his house where his wife, three daughters, and mother were alone. Since I expected that, I was prepared for it. Like I usually was.

I delivered the orders, which were clear and concise. I wanted every guard dead and the women brought to me at the safe house before sunrise. My men knew that if they let me down, it would only mean death for them, so I was sure they would deliver. After sending them on their way, Hector and I got ourselves comfortable and prepared to wait.

As the sun peeked through the windows of the safe house, my men were pulling up with Miguel's family just as I'd asked. Each of the women was led into the house bound, gagged, and blindfolded. I smiled at the handiwork of my men as I took out my phone and called Adriana.

"Papa!" she spoke as she answered the phone.

"Go!" I said while I waited for her to proceed.

There was ringing coming from the call she added before Miguel answered.

"Who is this?" Miguel said as he answered the phone.

"Adriana," Adriana said, putting on the thick Spanish accent she had picked up after all the time she'd spent with me.

"Ahhh, Adriiii, you must have found your daughter's body," he said, letting out a laugh.

Adriana and I were both amused and returned his laughter.

"I must say, you inherited a lot from your father but lack his common sense," I said, interrupting the gloating match that I was sure was going to take place between him and Adriana.

I walked over to Miguel's oldest daughter and slapped her before placing the phone to her ear and removing the cloth that muffled her sounds.

"*Papi!*" she screamed out into the phone.

I quickly hung up, giving Adriana the lead to complete things on her end. I looked back at Hector, who sat quietly with a machete on his lap. I smirked as I approached him and lifted it up. Under normal circumstances, his daughters would have been free to go. Unfortunately for them, there was nothing normal about the hell Miguel has caused my family.

I returned to where the five ladies were sitting and, one by one, beheaded them. Their heads rolled down their bodies and onto the floor. I handed the machete back to Hector.

"Clean this mess, package their heads, and leave the boxes on Miguel's property. Hector, get us a flight back to the States," I said before heading to my room to shower.

Adriana

After my father hung up the phone. I recited an address to Miguel and told him he had an hour to show if he wanted to save his precious family. The address was one of the warehouses that Cameron told us they had access to in Red Hook. It was the perfect remote location for what I had planned.

I was sitting in the security room of another one of Cameron's spots. This room had ongoing video footage of the various spots he had across the city. There was one screen I was watching intently. When I graduated from Howard, I thought I was going to put this life behind me for good. It was my intention, and I was doing a great job at sticking to it. However, once my daughter became heavily involved, there was no way I could stand back and watch it happen. Especially when this all could have been avoided if I'd killed Miguel right along with his father. Ricardo was my first kill, and I was so nervous about getting away with it that I wasn't concerned about getting rid of his young son. If I had known Miguel would grow to be a huge thorn in my child's side, I would have. I couldn't cry over spilled milk. All I could do was rectify the situation, which I fully planned on doing.

My thoughts were interrupted as I watched four SUVs pull up to the warehouse. All the men jumped out with their guns drawn and ready to blast anyone who was there. Too bad they would be rushing into an empty space. I let out a hearty laugh as I watched Miguel exit the last truck and enter the building.

I waited a few minutes to ensure that they were all inside, and when I didn't see any more men exit the SUVs, I proceeded with the plan. I hit the intercom button that was under the screen I was watching and began to speak.

"Welcome. Please have your men put down their weapons, Miguel," I spoke before hitting the next button to listen.

"Fuck you, cunt bitch! Where is my family?" Miguel spat.

I smiled inwardly and pressed the intercom once again. "I'm a woman of my word. You are going to see them right now," I said as I pressed the button on the detonator that was in my left hand.

I sat back and watched the building blow to pieces. The C-4 that was strategically placed by Cameron's boys was enough to bring the entire building down. I watched as it went up in flames, and I leaned back with a satisfactory smirk on my face.

Chapter Sixteen

Ty

Vic was released from the hospital a week after she gave birth to TJ. Even though she wasn't a patient anymore, we both were practically still residents between checking on Skye and staying with TJ from the start of visiting hours until they were over. Pop Pop, Hector, and Adriana handled the Mexicans. We didn't get many details on what went down, but we didn't need the details. If they said it was handled, then it was. All Cam and I had to do was focus on nursing the girls back to health and checking on TJ's progress. Doing that was nothing to us. Shit was actually going good until Aaliyah threw a monkey wrench in and put Cam on game about Man planning on setting him up. I didn't trust shorty, and even though she claimed she didn't want parts, deep down I knew she was just as shady as her cousin.

Man was lightweight, so he wasn't really a priority in terms of us getting at him ASAP. We still controlled his blocks, and he couldn't do shit about that unless he had the United States Army behind him. He didn't, so that bitch-ass nigga couldn't do nothing but keep calm until we brought the heat to him.

My main focus was my li'l nigga. TJ was getting stronger and stronger, and I couldn't be happier about that. I was worried that my boy wouldn't make it, but there he was nearly a month later and his progress was great. Little nigga was spoiled and had so much love around him. It's like the baby fever started spreading, because shortly after all that shit went down, Cam slipped up and told me Skye was pregnant again. I didn't understand why it was a secret until he told me her doctor said the baby might not make it. Skye was healing, and her unborn seed was thriving. Shit was cool on the family front.

Vic ended up coming clean about getting a private investigator to find my mom. Although I was pissed off with her from keeping that shit from me, I knew her heart was in the right place. I didn't want to confront my mom at all, nor did I want to hear what I felt like would have been a boatload of excuses, but after talking it through with Vic and Mariah, I decided maybe it wasn't such a bad idea. I surprised her at the hospital with flowers and offered to take her to lunch. Niggas couldn't tell me that she wasn't going to turn me down, but she didn't.

We kicked it at Olive Garden, and she held no punches. According to her, my father was married when she started fucking with him, and when she found out she was pregnant and confronted him and his wife about it, he said he wanted full custody and for her to disappear. Of course, my mom wasn't with that, but that's when the death threats and random ass whoopings started happening. She knew that the only way she would be able to keep her life was to give me to my father and his wife.

When I was just a few months old, my father's wife left him, which was why I had no recollection of the bitch whatsoever. My moms thought that, since she was out of the picture, my pops would let her back in my life, but he didn't. The threats against her life continued, and every time she showed up, she left with bruises to show for it. Eventually, she gave up but didn't leave the country like he told her to. She knew that one day she would be able to be in my life and didn't mind settling for watching over me from a distance if it meant that it would happen. She didn't expect it to take as many years as it did, but she was happy that it happened.

At first, I thought her story was a bit shaky until the next few times we linked up and she showed me letters she had written to my dad, asking to see me, and the letters he wrote back, cursing her out and threatening to kill her each time.

I was a dad and starting my own family. Why not give my moms the opportunity to be a part of TJ's life in ways she couldn't be there for me? If I was starting fresh, I had to start completely fresh. Couldn't pick and choose. I ended up welcoming her into my life, and so did the rest of the family. I even got to meet my little sister, who was a Mini-Me.

The ringing of my cell phone brought me out of my own head. "Yo," I answered without checking to see who was calling.

"Ty," my mother spoke, bringing a smile to my face.

"Wassup, Ma?" I asked. It was weird as fuck calling her Ma, but it made her smile, and to be honest, it felt good as shit to me.

"I was calling to check on TJ's progress. I know he's still progressing, but it wouldn't feel right if I didn't check," she said, sounding concerned.

"He good. Getting better and better every day," I said, sounding like the proud father I was.

We kicked it for a minute about everything under the sun. That was something I had gotten used to. Moms was cool as fuck. We could kick it about sports, music, video games, and of course, the minor relationship problems I would have with Vic. Like I wanted her to be there my entire life, she was finally able to be. It felt so right.

Skye

Since I had been home from the hospital, I had been spending a lot of time with my mother. Since everything that had gone down, when I found out about her ties to Pop Pop's organization, I felt we needed to get to know each other for real. Just like I always knew, we were no different. She did all the things she had done in her past to protect her family and those she cared about. Those were my exact reasons, so how could I be mad at her? It didn't take me long to forgive her for that, but getting over the fact that Hector was my father was a different hurdle.

One night while I was at Pop Pop's house on Staten Island, I called my mom and dad over so that we could all sit down. In order for me to get over the situation, I needed answers. Not an answer that would beat around the bush, but a "straight, no chaser" type answer. Although I'd spoken to my mom and dad separately and heard their separate versions of how it all went down, I needed them all together. The only way we were going to be able to move forward was together. Finally, they granted me that. Whatever I asked, they answered. No ifs, ands, or buts were included.

I learned that my mother and father were on a little break during the summer when my mother met and slept with Hector in Panama. When she found out she was pregnant with me, she let them both know. She didn't want anything from Hector outside of the little time they spent together during the summer, and she was planning a life with my dad, Harvey. The three of them agreed that a DNA test was not needed and that Harvey would be the only father I ever knew. Hector cared for me from a distance, though. He sent money often, which was never touched until I was given access to my account at 18. All the money I thought came from my parents was really from Hector. My mother ended up getting the DNA test done with just Hector because she didn't want to hurt my father's feelings. Her reason was that she knew it would come out one day, and when it did, she wanted to have definitive results to go. No maybes. I had already heard that all from my dad when we spoke while I was in the hospital. However, getting the same facts from all three of them made it all better in a weird way.

I accepted Hector into my life with ease because since I had met him, he had been in my corner through it all when he really didn't have to be. Harvey would always be my father. No DNA result could ever change that. Now that everything was on the table, he respected the relationship I wanted to have with Hector, and Hector promised not to step on his toes.

Cameron and I were back together, and our relationship had grown stronger than I ever imagined. The Cameron I met and fell in love with was back 1,000 percent, and I couldn't have been prouder of the man he had become due to the laundry list of peaks and valleys we had encountered. Neither of us was perfect, but our flaws were what made us perfect for each other. Throughout everything we had been through, I couldn't have seen myself going through it with anyone else. I just hoped that things stayed on this right path.

Chapter Seventeen

Ty

Cam and I were cruising through SoHo down Broadway. The plan was to hit up a few spots to get the women in our lives, Skye and Vic, something special just to show them how much we appreciated them for holding us down through all the bullshit that'd been going on. We wanted them to feel loved since they both had gone through some tough shit the past few months. TJ was home and doing well, and Skye was at a point in her pregnancy she hadn't thought she would reach. They deserved the world and more.

I was getting ready to park when Cam tapped me on my shoulder to get my attention. I looked over at him, and he pointed in the direction of the Prada store. I turned in the direction he was pointing and spotted Man.

"What the fuck!" I exclaimed, mad as hell, but nothing could compare to the look on Cam's face. He looked like he was ready to kill that nigga right then and there. Cam's hand was on the door, and he was about to hop out when I stopped him.

"Nah, Ty. I'm not tryin'a hear that. You coming or not? I been waiting too long not to take this opportunity!" Cam shouted with a look of rage in his eyes.

I had to admit we had been waiting too long, and that nigga Man just kept getting away somehow. But we couldn't just run up in the store and shoot the shit up. That wasn't our style, and it never would be.

"Look, bro, I know. Let's just wait 'til he come out, though, and follow him. Knowing that nigga, he probably going to hide out at some bitch house," I said, trying to reason with Cam. I was ready to end that nigga's life too, but doing it in public just wasn't a good idea. I could tell by the look on his face and his tight grip on the door handle that Cam still wasn't sold on the idea of waiting.

"You not thinking this shit through. It's four of them niggas to two of us. What if something happens to me or you because you decided to just rush up in that bitch like SWAT and take matters into your own hands? What I'ma tell Skye and your moms if you don't make it because I went along with this shit? I ain't tryin'a let you die today, and it definitely ain't my day to go either," I continued to plead my case.

With the words I'd just spat at Cam, he was starting to feel my idea a lot better. His tight-ass grip on the door loosened, and he turned in his seat, looking straight ahead with his jaw tight.

"A'ight, we gon' do this your way, but this nigga gotta die today. I'm tired of niggas thinking they can test me and get away with the shit," Cam replied.

He was serious as hell and ready to get this shit done and over with. *Let the games begin.*

Cameron

At least forty-five minutes had lapsed, and that nigga was still in the store. You would have thought he spotted us and was hiding out. That wasn't likely, though. I was getting antsier by the minute. I had so much rage built up for this nigga Man it wasn't even funny. If you could kill a nigga and kill him again, I would do that to Man, no questions asked. I was about to say fuck it and just get out of the car and go alone and kill him if I had to. That's when I spotted Man and his crew coming out of the store with shopping bags. Ty looked over at me as he started the car back up.

"You ready to do this?" Ty asked.

"Hell yeah," I said, looking over at the truck that started moving with Man and his crew inside. Ty knew I had been waiting for a while to catch this nigga Man, so I don't even know why he asked that question.

As we took off following close but not too close behind Man and his crew, I couldn't help but think if I should let that bitch nigga die a slow death or just end it with a bullet to the head. Ty looked over and saw the small but present grin on my face.

"Tell me you thinking what I'm thinking," Ty stated.

I laughed because I already knew what my nigga was thinking without even having to question it. "Yeah, how we gon' kill this nigga? I say let him die a slow, painful death then shoot him," I said.

"I agree," Ty replied.

As we followed Man and them, I noticed we ended up in Brownsville. It was the hood, so when we killed Man, the boys wouldn't come right away. Reaching into the glove compartment, I pulled out my nine and put the silencer on it. I took out gloves that were tucked behind my nine, handed Ty a pair, and slipped on a pair of my own.

Man had finally made it to his destination and hopped out of the car, grabbing some bags. When his crew didn't, I knew we were at the house of one of Man's bitches or somebody who was close to him. This shit was going to be easier than I thought. We waited until the truck pulled off to put our plan into motion. I watched intently as Man knocked on the door. Shortly after, he was greeted with a kiss by some chick neither I nor Ty knew. Nigga came to get ass. Too bad it wouldn't get that far. Once they were both inside, Ty and I jumped out of the whip.

Deciding not to waste another minute, Ty knocked on the door like it was nothing and he was expected. I had my nine aimed at the door, not giving a fuck, ready to blast whoever opened it. The games were over. We played the cat-and-mouse game for too long with this nigga. It was all coming to an end that day.

When the door swung open, I couldn't believe who it was. Aaliyah. She had a smile on her face, but when she saw this shit wasn't a social call, it faded instantly. She probably wouldn't have had any worries if she hadn't lied to me. She talked a good game when she told me Man was tryin'a set me up. All that "I'm done with him, Cam. I'm not fucking with him like that, family or not" shit was bull.

Ty and I both knew she was going to attempt to run, but we couldn't have that. Ty quickly grabbed her and put his hand over her mouth to muffle her noises. Not even giving it a second thought, I put a bullet right in the middle of her eyes, killing her instantly. Ty laid her on the carpet and closed the door.

Good thing I had the silencer on my piece. I didn't want to alarm our target that we were on the scene. We followed Man's voice and the other bitch's voice, and that led us into the living room. I aimed my gun and pulled the trigger, causing the girl's head to explode. No words needed to be shared. I wasn't there to give a speech, nor did I want to listen to one. Man thought he was slick and tried to go for his gun. I halted that by letting one off, hitting him in his kneecap.

"Ahhh, shit!" Man screamed out, grabbing his knee.

Was I supposed to feel guilty? Fuck no. I walked over to him and kicked him dead in the knee I just shot. I heard it crack and felt even better looking on as he screamed out like a little bitch. Ty was laughing his ass off at that nigga.

"Tell me something, Man. You thought you was gonna do all the shit you did and get away with it?" I spat, not really giving a fuck if he answered the question.

Man just looked on with hate dancing around in his eyes. I expected more of a reaction. I needed more. It'd been a long time coming, and this nigga was tryin'a going out on some bitch shit. I drew back my hand and threw a left hook that connected with his jaw.

"Man up, bitch," I shouted, watching as he grabbed his jaw. "Yo, bro, go grab me a knife out the kitchen. I got a surprise for this nigga," I stated.

Man's eyes got big as shit once he realized how real it was about to get. I had to laugh, because that nigga really was bitch made.

Man

There was a fiery, throbbing sensation in my knee. Shit hurt like hell. I watched as Ty handed the knife to that bitch-ass nigga Cam. How the fuck did these niggas catch me slipping like this? I didn't know what he was about to do, but I had to think quickly. I wasn't trying to give up without a fight. I tried to rise up off the couch and was stopped by a gunshot to my other knee.

"Fuck you!" I screamed out in pain.

I felt tears come to my eyes because the pain was becoming unbearable. I wasn't ready to die, but I knew that was Cam's end game. I just wished the nigga got it over with. My eyes widened as Cam raised the knife and slowly began to slide it across the skin on my chest. I'd never been in so much pain in my life. I closed my eyes as he continued to inflict pain by making slashes across my chest. The blood began to flow from the cuts, and I couldn't do a damn thing about it. When I did try to fight it, I started to feel lightheaded.

"Cam, end it. Let's get low," I heard Ty say.

Cam shook his head up and down and stepped closer to me. Slowly he started to slit my throat. I reached up and grabbed my throat and felt the blood oozing from it. I couldn't scream or do shit. I was dying slowly and painfully. I prayed the nigga would just end it. After watching the life leave my body for a few minutes, he finally decided it was time. I watched Cam raise the gun until it was level with my head. I closed my eyes and began to ask God to forgive me for all the shit I'd ever done.

Cameron

I pulled the trigger and watched the bullet enter his skull, and his lifeless body slumped over. Man was the last piece of the ongoing string of bullshit that had been occurring in my life this past year. It was finally over. I looked over at Ty, who confirmed that he was thinking the exact same thing I was thinking. All he had to do was nod.

We didn't waste any more time lingering around and left undetected. During the ride back to my crib, we kicked it about everything that had transpired since I met Skye. We made it and really couldn't understand why. The life we lived guaranteed only two exit options: cuffs or a coffin. Yet there we were free and alive. We both knew it was time to get shit right.

We were family men. Ty had Vic and TJ, I had Skye, Cairo, and our baby girl on the way, whom we decided we would name Faith. Thinking about where we started and how we had grown brought me to the realization that we needed to be over this shit. It wasn't a necessity anymore. My dad wasn't here, so I had nothing to prove to him. My family had bread that would last longer than

I would probably live, so that wasn't an issue either. There was nothing keeping either of us in the game, and the more we spoke about it out loud, the more realized it.

As we pulled up to the crib, we made a vow to each other that the Man situation was it. We were putting the past in the past and looking at a much brighter future. I knew what my next step would be, and with Skye's birthday coming up, I knew exactly when I was going to take it.

Chapter Eighteen

Skye

I walked into Rose Castle and was bombarded with a giant surprise. I told Cameron and my parents that I didn't want a party, but of course they didn't listen. I felt like a whale and was always ready for a nap. Who could possibly enjoy a party under those conditions? I didn't want them to feel bad about their surprise, so I put on my poker face and greeted each "happy birthday" I received with a thank-you and a smile.

"You like?" Cameron said, running up behind me and placing his hands on my stomach.

"I do. You really didn't have to go through all of this. I was totally fine with a nice, intimate dinner with just the family," I said, turning to face him so that he could give me a kiss. I puckered my lips to him, and he leaned over and placed his succulent lips on mine.

"I know that, but you deserve this. I love you," he said before Victoria approached us, giving him the chance to get away.

"Happy birthday, old lady!" Victoria said, pulling me in for a hug.

"Thanks, Vic. Where is my baby? I see bad-ass Cairo running around. He's usually attached to whoever has TJ," I said while laughing.

"He was. Mom is over there with him, but he fell asleep. Soon as he was knocked out, Cairo dipped on her," Victoria said, joining me in laughter.

I had to admit that although I hadn't wanted a party, it was turning out to be a great evening. It has been so long since everyone could get together and party like we had no worries, and it felt good having that opportunity. It was nice to see both my dads and my mom there getting along. Pop Pop had returned as well so he wouldn't miss it. Everyone who was near and dear to me was present, which included the select few of Cameron and Ty's homeboys we considered family.

The night was amazing, and I honestly didn't think it could have gotten any better. I should have known, though, when it came to Cameron.

"Attention!" Cameron shouted while standing on the stage in the middle of the room with a mic in his hand.

My eyes locked with his, and he motioned for me to join him on stage. I really didn't want to get up from the seat I was in because my feet were killing me. I also didn't want to ruin whatever it was he had planned, so I got my fat butt up and wobbled over to the stage. He took my hand and helped me up the steps before continuing to address the guests.

"First off, I want to thank you all for coming out and celebrating my baby's birthday with us. I could never really thank you all enough for making this a night she really deserves." Cameron turned to me and kissed me on my forehead.

"Skye, from the day you bumped into me, I knew you were the woman I would spend the rest of my life with. Real shit, everything about you screamed 'forever.' You're intelligent, hella beautiful, driven, and sassy as shit. I can't forget that you're definitely a rider. I couldn't have picked a better woman to share my life with, let alone bear my children. I appreciate you and everything you encompass. I love you with every fiber of my being, and I know this type of love will never die. I'm content and extremely happy with the way things are now, but it could get better. In order for that to happen, we gotta do it right," Cameron stated before retrieving a small ring box and dropping down to one knee.

He opened the ring box, and my eyes fell on the most beautiful princess-cut canary ring. A smile spread across my face as he continued to speak.

"So here, in front of all our family and friends, I'm hoping that you don't embarrass a nigga and turn me down." Everyone laughed. "Nah, but seriously, let's do it right. For Cairo, for Faith, and for the true love that we share. Will you marry me?" Cameron asked with a grin wide as the equator.

It took a minute for me to respond. Not because I was thinking about my answer, but because I was taking in the moment. I looked to my right and saw my mom and Mariah both wiping the tears away that escaped during Cameron's proposal, and then I turned back to him.

"Of course I will, Cameron. I love you so much!" I shouted as he stood and pulled me in for a kiss.

The entire hall erupted into cheers, and people were shouting congrats left and right. As I stood in his embrace, I quickly reflected on everything that led up to that moment. Whether it had been good or bad, it was worth it.

Chapter Nineteen

Cameron

Eight Months Later

I recall when we first met, a long time ago
How could I forget the way I felt
When I first laid eyes on you
Gerald Levert's smooth baritone voice sang as the tune of "Made to Love Ya" began to play, signaling that it was finally the moment I'd been waiting for since the day I met her. I looked straight ahead, holding my breath. Finally, I was able to breathe when I saw the love of my life appear at the top of the flower-filled walkway. She was accompanied by both of her fathers. Harvey and Hector wore smiles on their faces bright enough to light the darkest room. They made slow strides down the aisle while Gerald's voice serenaded the crowd filled with those closest to us.

I have everything I ever wanted, I thought, looking over to where Adriana sat holding my baby girl, Faith. Right beside her was my prince, Cairo. He sat swinging his legs and staring intently at his mom as she made her way toward me. Everything we'd been through leading up to that moment was all worth it if this was the outcome. I only planned on doing the marriage thing once, and a nigga was proud as hell that it was with Skye.

When she finally came to a stop in front of me, I reached out and held her hands in mine.

Skye

Feeling his touch still gave me butterflies. Standing before and preparing to take vows in front of God, our family, and friends was a surreal moment. Who would have thought that after all the trials our relationship had endured, we would make it to this moment? I was the little girl who dreamed of a huge fairytale-type wedding, and it was all there, I was marrying my soul mate, and we had two beautiful children. Having Cairo and Faith really solidified my relationship with Cameron. Our children bought out the best in us and had us wanting to do right for them and for ourselves. I had them to thank for this moment.

I thought about the life Cameron and I planned to have with the kids as the preacher began the ceremony.

"Dearly beloved, we are gathered here today on this very happy and joyous occasion to join Cameron and Skye in holy matrimony. Marriage is a solemn institution to be held in honor by all. It is the cornerstone of the family. It requires of those who undertake it a complete and unreserved giving of one's self. It is not to be entered into lightly, as marriage is a sincere and mutual commitment to love one another. This commitment symbolizes the intimate sharing of two lives and still enhances the individuality of each of you," he pronounced.

As he spoke, I couldn't help but imagine the future Cameron and I would have with our children. My babies meant the world and more to me, and I couldn't thank Cameron enough for assisting me in bringing them into the world. My life was finally how I saw it. It was really happening. I felt a rush of blood, which felt as if it were forming puddles in my cheek, and I knew I was blushing. Thank goodness my face was still hidden behind the veil.

"Cameron, do you take Skye to be your wedded wife? Do you promise to love her, comfort her, honor and keep her in sickness and in health, remaining faithful to her as long as you both shall live?" the pastor said, bringing to my attention to this, the moment that dreams were made of.

I looked at Cameron as he began to move his succulent lips. I couldn't wait to kiss them once again. We had been separated for three whole days, and I was yearning for a kiss from my love.

"I do!" Cameron shouted, causing a low giggle to flow through the crowd. He was anxious, and it was obvious. I couldn't front. I was too. There we were, one step away from being Mr. and Mrs. Carter. "Surreal" was an understatement in terms of how I felt about that moment. Nonetheless, I was extremely happy and felt extremely blessed.

"Skye, do you take Cameron to be your wedded husband? Do you promise to love him, comfort him, honor and keep him in sickness and in health, remaining faithful to him as long as you both shall live?" the pastor said, turning his attention to me.

I felt like jumping up and down and screaming, of course. However, I needed to contain my excitement . . . at least for a few more minutes.

"I do," I said, fighting back the urge to cry.

There were a few more words delivered by the pastor, and before I knew it, I was in Cameron's arms, on the receiving end of the most passionate kiss we had ever shared. I didn't know if it was because I'd been wanting it for three long days or because it was just that intense. A mixture of both, I supposed.

The crowd of our guests erupted in applause as I intertwined my arm with Cameron's and jumped the broom. Not lasting any more than an hour, my ceremony was everything I'd dreamt it to be and more. Departing the area where my ceremony was held was when I had the chance to really bask in the beauty of the venue. Cipriani was very sophisticated. It was set in an Italian Renaissance theme with towering columns, a soaring ceiling, and gorgeous inlaid floors. It was everything I'd dreamed of since I was a young girl.

We were led to the area where our reception was being held and shared our first dance. Mariah Carey and Luther Vandross's "Endless Love" boomed throughout the room as my husband and I danced. I was so focused on him that everyone else in the room became invisible. I was on a cloud, one that I never wanted to come down from.

"I love you, Mrs. Carter," Cameron whispered in my ear before twirling me into the arms of my father. It was time for the father-daughter dance.

"I love you more, Mr. Carter," I yelled above Beyoncé's "Daddy."

I shared the dance with both of my fathers, and neither of them seemed to mind. It probably was a bit unorthodox, but I couldn't say that I would have rather had it any other way. Girls were lucky and blessed to have one father, but I was beyond that. I had two who loved me dearly, and that made the moment all that more special.

The sentimental moments were coming to an end, and the reception was underway. I held Faith in my arms while we danced with the two most important men in our life: Cairo and Cameron. Things were going great, and everyone was having an amazing time. I was all smiles until a dark, gloomy feeling came over me.

Taking notice, Cameron pulled me to the side to inquire about my change in mood. "Baby, what's wrong?" he said, looking extremely concerned.

"I don't know. I just had this feeling come over me. Something isn't right," I stated, staring deep into his eyes.

Faith was squirming in my arms, so I bounced her gently to calm her down. That worked like a charm.

"Everything is perfect. Look around," he said, flashing me a reassuring smile.

I took his advice and scanned the room of our loved ones. That's when I spotted what wasn't right. I was too late. All I remembered was gunfire erupting and catastrophe taking place. Cameron pulled Cairo, Faith, and me into the corner and ran toward the pandemonium while retrieving two Colts from the inside of his tuxedo jacket.

"Noooo, Cameron!" I screamed out over the gunfire.

Faith was now throwing a fit of piercing screams, which trickled down to Cairo as well. Cairo was crouched down in the corner with his hands over his ears, calling for his dad over and over. As bad as I wanted to run after Cameron, my children were the priority. I pulled them close to me and used my body as a shield. It brought back memories of when I was shot, but I shook my thoughts off. The gunfire seemed to be never ending. All I could think about was how the best day of my life had turned into a giant nightmare.

After what seemed like forever, the gunfire finally ceased. All that could be heard were screams. I was afraid to move, not for me but because of my babies. Although the gunfire had stopped, I hadn't a clue if it would start again. I couldn't risk it.

"Come on, sis," Ty said as he reached us. He helped me up from the crouching position I was in and took Faith out of my arms.

"I'm not leaving Cameron," I cried.

"He will be fine. Please trust me and let's go," Ty barked.

I hesitated for a second before grabbing Cairo and following Ty. Once we were outside, Ty led us to the limo where Victoria and TJ were, and he opened the door.

"Get in. Y'all leaving," he said.

I looked from the limo back to Cipriani and back to the limo again. I kissed Cairo and ushered him into the limo before pecking Faith on her forehead and running back into the building.

Cameron

This shit was out of control. *I knew these Mexican motherfuckers would try to retaliate for Miguel's death, but why did it have to be today?* I thought as I assessed the scene. I was looking for my wife and my kids, and my mother too. I really just needed to see that my son and daughter were straight. Among the cold bodies were a bunch of dead Mexicans. *Good for their bitch asses,* I thought as I continued to look. None belonged to any of my family, so I thought I was straight. I thought entirely too fast. As soon as I hit the corner, I walked up on a scene I wished I could have gone back in time to correct.

I walked closer, not believing that this was real when I heard my name called.

"Cameron." I turned to see Skye quickly approaching me.

I was screaming for her to stop and turn around, but the words weren't coming out. I was in shock. She got closer, and I looked down at the scene before me and back to her. *Don't come over here, baby.* I couldn't verbalize the words for shit. I was too late.

The moment she walked up near me and got a better look at what I saw, she fell to her knees and let out a gut-wrenching scream.

"Mommmmy," she screamed out as she crawled over to where Adriana lay motionless in the arms of Harvey.

Pop Pop was beside Harvey on the floor, applying pressure to her wounds in an attempt to stop the bleeding. It was impossible. There was blood running from a hole in her chest and one on the side of her head. Her eyes were open, and they were lifeless.

"Mommy, please, get up! I need you, Mom, please. Cai and Faith need you," Skye cried, leaning over and pulling Adriana closer to her.

I bent down and attempted to pick her up to take her away, but she swung violently and continued to scream. Sirens could be heard, and I was carrying. Leaving Skye wasn't an option, so I took off my tux jacket and held the gun as I wiped the prints with my shirt. Still holding it with my jacket, I put it down and kicked it away from me. My attempts to remove Skye from Adriana's body were useless. It pained me in a way I couldn't explain to watch Skye break down. I knew the feeling all too well since I, too, had lost a parent. I wouldn't have wished that pain on a random-ass person, so it killed me watching Skye go through it.

Police arrived on the scene as well as paramedics, and that's when we were finally able to separate Skye from Adriana.

"No, let me go!" Skye screamed and kicked, trying to break free from my grasp. I pulled her closer and tightened the grip I had on her. She sank into my chest and sobbed.

"Why my mom?" Skye cried as I rubbed her back.

"I'm sorry, baby, I really am. I got you, though. You're not alone. We will get through this together," I said.

It didn't matter how genuine I was. Nothing I said would heal her pain or fill the void. It would take a while, but I had every intention of holding her hand the entire way.

Chapter Twenty

Skye

The burial was over, and I watched everyone take slow strides to their cars. I wouldn't move. I couldn't even if I wanted to. This was my last chance to say goodbye to my mother, and I was still unable to believe that it really was happening. She was supposed to be here to help me with Cairo and Faith. She was supposed to be here for me to cry on her shoulder when Cameron and I went through our issues. She was never supposed to leave me.

"Why did you leave me, Mommy?" I inquired as I fell to my knees and sobbed before her plot.

I didn't care that I was in a dress, on my knees in the dirt. My mother was gone. There would be no more girls' days spent shopping and going to the spa. No more girl talk. Nothing! All I was left with were memories. I wanted and needed more. I looked up and spotted Cameron walking toward me. He had left my side for a minute just to take Cairo and Faith to the limo. He was stopped by Hector. After the two shared a few words, Hector walked away from Cameron and headed in my direction. Cameron didn't move, though. He stood there looking at me, ready to rush to my side if need be.

I was engulfed in sobbing and saying out loud that I wished it were all a nightmare and that I would wake up any minute when I felt Hector's arm go around my shoulder as he fell on his knees and pulled me close to him.

"Let it out, Skye," Hector said as he rubbed my back.

I sobbed into his shoulder and asked over and over why my mother left me. "She was everything to me. Why? I'm alone now. It wasn't supposed to be like this. It's my fault. I should have listened when she told me not to pursue handling Cameron's business. She would be here if I didn't. My mom is gone," I cried out.

"This is in no way your fault. You are not alone. You have Cam, you have your beautiful children, your grand-father, Harvey, and you have me. You are surrounded by so many people who love you. We will help you through this. You don't have to try to be strong for everyone anymore. It's our turn to be strong for you, and we will," Hector tried to assure me.

"Dad is so out of tune with everything. I need to be there for him and help him. Pop Pop already made plans to leave, and you will be leaving too. Everything is so messed up."

"Your father needs time. Just like you, he is hurting and trying to cope with the loss of his wife. We are here for him too. Believe me. Harvey and I don't always see eye to eye, but I got love for him. He's raised you. How could I not? Your grandfather is leaving because he has to. I, on the other hand, will not leave you. Not like this. I haven't been here for a lot of things, but this I will definitely see you through. Don't worry about that," Hector said as he helped me up.

Cameron saw that Hector helped me up, and he scurried to my side. I threw myself into his arms, and he squeezed me, letting me know that he had me. He scooped me into his arms and carried me toward our limo. I looked over his shoulder and whispered goodbye to my mom. It wouldn't be an easy journey, but at the same time, the best thing for myself and those around me was for me to start looking toward the future.

Epilogue

Since the death of her mother, Skye had become a completely different person. She wasn't cold or frigid as you would expect someone to be after suffering such a great loss. Her view on life was different. She felt as if losing her mother was the ultimate price she had to pay for all the wrong she had done. It was also her chance for the fresh start she always voiced that she wanted.

Finding her way back to church after many years of not attending a service, her healing journey had begun. She was no longer interested in anything related to the street. Her only interest was being the best mother she could be to Cairo and Faith. She completed her studies and earned her Juris Doctor degree, which was the first step to taking over and successfully running her mother's law firm.

She wasn't where she would have liked to be emotionally, but she was getting there. It wasn't a journey she had to endure alone. There was the constant help of her father, her grandfather, and the love of her life. Although Pop Pop had returned to Panama, he made it a priority to stay involved in the lives of Skye and her kids. Hector kept his promise and stayed behind, although he took frequent trips back home.

As promised, Cameron kept his word to Skye and refrained from running the street. After all the losses they'd suffered and sacrifices they'd made collectively, he finally arrived at the realization that none of it was worth it. He had his children, his wife, and more than enough money to last them a lifetime. He, too, had completed school and possessed a Juris Doctor degree. He ended up getting a job offer to work at Harvey's sports agent firm, where he was now a partner. In his spare time, he picked up the niche of writing and penned a few titles based on his and Skye's life. In addition to work, he was focused on being a loving and doting father to his children as well as a husband to Skye.

Since TJ was a little older, Victoria finally kept her promise to Skye and went to school. She got a degree in nursing and had started working at Miami University Hospital under Skye's grandparents. She and Ty moved back there shortly after their wedding to give TJ the taste of a different life besides city life. Victoria was pretty content with her new life, but the allure of the street calling her was a battle she fought every day. You know what they say: old habits die hard.

Ty's chance to be the boss finally presented itself. He didn't need to cross his longtime friend to get there, either. With Cameron completely out of the game, his empire was up for grabs. Who else would be better suited than the one who was there from the start? However, after the dust had settled, even Ty wanted more. After moving back to Miami, he decided to go into business with Pop Pop. Legit business! They ended up opening a club and restaurant right in South Beach. His relationship with his mother had evolved tremendously, and eventually, she and his little sister joined Ty and Victoria in Miami. Even though Ty felt that his wife, son, and in-laws were the only family he really needed, at the end of the day, he finally felt complete once Erica and his sister entered his life.

Pop Pop had the business in Miami with Ty, but he still had an organization to run. He returned to Panama a few months after Adriana's death to resume his business.

He visited often enough to touch base with Ty and spend time with Skye and her kids.

For Hector, going back to Panama wasn't an option. Although he still respected the relationship Skye had with Harvey, he didn't want to leave her. The secret was out, so he planned on being 100 percent active in her life. There was money to be made in the States, and with Cam out of business and leaving a team of money-hungry young boys to fend for themselves, Hector picked up the slack. So essentially, it was business as usual for him. He just got a chance to be near his daughter and grandkids.

The crew learned the hard way that everyone has an agenda, whether it be good or bad. Everyone wants to be in some position of power. There's nothing wrong with that. It's what you do to achieve your position that defines you as a person.

A sneak preview of

Shorty Gotta Be Grown

by

T.C. Littles

On sale July 2020

Shorty Gotta Be Grown

by

T.C. Littles

Dedication

By the end of this story, you're all going to have MUCH RESPECT and MUCH LOVE for Calvin Jackson. The same way I have MUCH LOVE, RESPECT, AND ADMIRATION for

Rodney Jones – the man behind the character. Yendor, this one is for YOU!

Chapter 1

Porsha

Snacking on a bag of Skittles, which was my favorite candy, I was sitting Indian style in front of the television, rolling a quarter of weed into blunts for my mother. She smoked like a choo-choo train, so I was always doing this chore for her. It was a regular day-to-day task. I loved it, though. Why? 'Cause I always broke off a few buds for me and my girl Imani to smoke on the low. That was just one benefit of having a trapping momma.

Telling my story, both my mother and father were trappers. My dad was a trapping king. My mom was his trap queen, so of course that made me the trap princess. Even my one-year-old brother was considered a trap prince by default. We were on some Momma Dee–type shit, thinking we had a royal place in the hood. Only thing was, weren't no lights flashing, cameras rolling, or a set of lines we'd remembered and rehearsed to survive. The drama that popped off around here wasn't scripted. Hell, most of the folks around here couldn't afford cable to watch reality television.

Digging the sugary pieces of candy out of my tooth, I was tuned into the sitcom on television like I hadn't seen the episode a million times. Being that I was home at least three and half days out of the week, I saw a lot of the same stuff they played over and over again. I wasn't complaining, though. I was lucky my parents didn't stress me about school. All my other peers were pushed out the house as soon as the sun rose because their parents didn't feel like being bothered. Around here, the schools were a joke, and the teachers only showed up to babysit. I learned more from being at home with my 'rents than I ever had in a stuffy classroom. Calvin and Trinity taught me the most important things in life—how to survive, make money, and get respect. Plus, they didn't need the school system babysitting me when they needed me to babysit Benzie.

Hearing my mother clear her throat, I broke my neck looking behind me. It got on my nerves when she crept up on me like an FBI agent, especially since she didn't come with a filter and popped off on me and whoever else for the simplest of things. Leaning in the doorway with tight lips and a ripped expression, it looked like she was thinking of way to irk me. Then she did.

"It's taking you a mighty long time to get finished, don't ya think?"

Even though I shouldn't have, I sucked my teeth before responding smartly, "Naw, not really. I'm almost done."

"You better watch how you respond, little girl," she warned, but I failed to take heed. I was too busy fixing my mouth to remind her I was almost grown.

"Little girl?" I questioned, sounding flabbergasted on purpose. "Naw to that too, Ma. I'm almost eighteen if you've forgotten." As soon as the words left my mouth, I regretted saying them. From the look on Trinity's face, I'd gone too far.

"Oh, hell naw, li'l bitch! I don't care how fat ya ass gets; you'll always be a little girl to me," she spat, just getting started. "And I know how old you'll be in a few weeks. I pushed yo' ass outta my pussy, and you better hope I don't stuff you back up in here. Keep talking."

My mom was going off on me, but she was the only one talking. I'd been gone into shut-down mode. All I did was stare and agree, taking the tongue lashing like a G, as I should've been since I'd been getting scolded since I quit babbling as a baby. Benzie was now getting the treatment I got at age one, though my mom was a little bit softer than she was in my toddler days.

"Yo' ass must've caught a helluva contact and lost your motherfucking mind up in here rolling my weed for you to be talking to me out the box like that." She was still going off. "I don't give a fuck how grown you think you are. I'll drag you all up and through this muthafuckin' house!"

Trinity might've been right. Naw, scratch that, I knew Trinity was right. Drunk or not, I'd be a fool to under-estimate her gangster. She'd bust you upside ya head with a glass in her hand and manage not to spill a drop. Trust and believe, I was all too familiar with her I-don't-give-a-fuck attitude, and I wasn't in the mood for an ass whooping. Especially since she had a fresh fifth of vodka off in her system.

Instead of responding, I turned back facing the TV and started packing as much weed as I could into one of the last cigarillos left. My fingers were moving faster than they did on Twitter so she wouldn't notice all the remain-ing buds in the bottom of the baggie. The quicker I could get the 'rello stuffed, sealed, and ready to be lit, the faster Trinity could push on about her way. At least that's what I'd assumed. My silence and what seemed like a complete disregard for Trinity's presence made matters worse.

"Um, you must want me to knock you in the back of your big-ass head or something," she barked.

"Huh? What?" It slipped off my tongue as it slid off the blunt wrapper from sealing it. Blinking, huffing, and puffing, I looked back at my mom with the stink face. "I ain't even didn't nothing for you to be riding me for, Ma."

I knew I should've been controlling myself, but I couldn't stop acting out. The same person that was grilling me about respect was the same person who passed her genes and behavior traits to act a damn fool down to me. She instilled this feistiness into me. I'd gotten this attitude honestly.

Leaning off the door frame, she came into my room and set her cup onto my dresser. I scooted back, recognizing the look of fury in my mom's eyes. I knew it all too well. Holding my breath, I waited for Trinity's reaction. I had a bad habit of learning my lesson after I'd taken things too far.

"When I tell you to shut your mouth and quit talking, I mean exactly that, Porsha. You ain't grown, you ain't tough, and you ain't gotta have no teeth in that mouth you keep running. Niggas love it when a bitch slobbing with all gums anyway. So, keep talkin', trying to match my gangster, and I'ma grow yo' baby ass all the way up" She cursed me out without remorse. Whenever Trinity went, please believe she went hard.

Just when I thought I'd dodged a bullet and was only gonna get verbally snapped on, she took three steps closer toward me and slapped me dead across my face. The blunt and buds of weed I was rolling up slipped from my fingers onto the floor. Tears gathered in my eyes, making my vision blurry as my head vibrated from the intensity of her blow. I should've never sent for my mother with my rebellious teenage attitude. My face was throbbing. It was painfully clear I wasn't ready for her comeback.

"If you quit running ya mouth like ya grown, I'll quit fuckin' ya young ass up," she schooled me. "You act like you're either dumb as fuck or smoking our product sometimes, Porsha. You should already know from seeing me go toe-to-toe with your father and a countless number of hood hoes that I'm not to be tried." After shaking her head like she was supremely disappointed in me, she continued. "Well, quit sitting there stuck still like there's not business to handle. Clean that shit up outta my carpet, go get your brother situated with his whining behind, and then go help your father."

With one hand gripping my stinging cheek, I jumped to complete her orders. Trinity wasn't about to get another problem out of me.

"Good girl." She mocked me nastily. "Keep that up and you won't get the life strangled up outta ya, or worse."

I took heed to Trinity's warning. I believed her threats. I swear to God I did.

Eventually reaching Benzie's room, my frown turned into a smile when I pushed the door open. His did too. All the crying and fussing he'd been doing immediately stopped as soon as he saw me. Begging to be picked up, my little brother was standing in his crib with his arms open wide and drool everywhere.

Benzie was spoiled rotten and a hellion already. Forget the Terrible Twos. Li'l man was wilding out at one. But with a family like ours, he got it honest.

My little brother and I were sixteen years apart but close as ever. I was more than just his big sister. I'd been caring for him since the day my parents brought him home. I hadn't been upset that I was no longer the only child. I'd been more so frustrated that his birth meant more responsibility for me. My mom claimed she was going through some type of postpartum depression bullshit causing her to drink, smoke, and stay under the covers with her eyes glued to the television all day, but she was like that before getting pregnant.

It was not a day of my childhood I didn't remember my momma drinking and smoking. The more money my dad made, the more she drank and got high. I couldn't wait until I got to break into the family business so my pockets wouldn't have a bottom either. I wasn't gonna have any kids, though. Helping raise Benzie ruined that.

Of course, there were days I hated looking after Benzie, pretending to be his mom and not his big sister. The responsibilities that weren't mine interfered with teenage antics I was looking to pull. But my dad was big on family. He felt, preached, and taught that we were supposed to hold each other down no matter what.

"We're all we've got in this cold and cruel world, Porsha. You better ride just as hard for Benzie, your mom, and me as I ride hard for you. No one in this family should fail if we keep each other's backs covered. Do you understand?"

My dad's words played over in my head just as clearly as when I'd heard him speak them. Since that day, I didn't complain about being my brother's keeper.

"Come here, bro-bro. Let me get you into a fresh diaper," I cooed at him, picking him up into a bear hug.

Benjamin reminded me of the baby dolls I used to play with as a kid. With a head full of curls, mocha-colored skin that was tanning into a shade that would probably be a rich brown chocolate like our father's, and bright brown eyes, he was the cutest baby ever—at least to me. His facial features were like Trinity's, similar to a pretty boy. But his expressions were like Calvin's, bold and uncaring. He was gonna be a muthafucka when he grew up, just as I was earning my stripes as one. We couldn't help it, being melting pots of Trin and Cal.

He went crazy wanting to play, so we did. He had every PlaySkool toy under the sun to keep him occupied, so I put a few of those in rotation while singing along with the interactive songs.

It was fun being a kid with my little brother, but I was in a rush to be grown for myself and my sanity. I'd done enough time in the trap and was ready to experience life on my own. Growing up under Calvin and Trinity could be a bit much. Benzie was lucky, though. He'd have me to seek refuge with. I actually liked having the li'l dude around.

"Tee-bee," Benzie babbled, pointing to the television.

"Okay," I replied slowly so he'd catch onto another word. It was fun teaching him how to talk and see him mimic things I did. The only downside was that I had to watch what I said and how I acted. The wrong repeated word could have my ass in a slang. The 'rents didn't play.

After turning on his favorite cartoon channel, I got him all the way together with some clean clothes, a few toys, and a hefty bottle full of oatmeal and applesauce. He was quiet, content, and all into an episode of *Paw Patrol* when I left him to go help our daddy.

Chapter 2

Porsha

Walking down two flights of stairs from the top floor of our home to the basement, I used my key to let myself in one of the doors. Our basement had three rooms: the washroom, bathroom, and recreation room that had a seating area as well as a kitchen. The rec room was where all the magic happened. This part of the house was not only where my father cooked and packaged his product, but also his man cave away from the world. It was decked out like the rest of our crib. There was a 60-inch projector screen TV inserted into the wall, five oversized leather chairs with cup holders built into them, and a fully functional kitchen that stayed stocked with beer and Remy.

On any random day, my dad and his crew would link up to cook at our house. That wasn't nothing compared to what went down on a daily basis, however. My parents were infamous for throwing gambling parties and smoke-out sessions. Those were the nights strippers came to perform and ended up tricking out in the open. Those parties only went down on the first floor.

Our house was originally a four-family flat, but my father purchased it from a coke head that was in debt to him. The guy signed over the deed to spare his life, and my father renovated the entire house and customized it to fit his trapping lifestyle. There were six bedrooms on each floor, four bathrooms, and a kitchen on each level that we only ate fast food in. He sometimes called it heaven and hell. The bottom floor was where all the madness unfolded, while the upstairs was sealed off for only me, him, Mom, and Benzie. My friends thought I was hella lucky to have such a huge house, but that was because they weren't the ones cleaning it from top to bottom.

"Hey, baby girl. Are you ready to help Daddy build up our empire?" he questioned, looking up from the concoction he was cooking up.

Whenever my dad hustled, he considered his risks to be investments for his family. Never once did he let the police turn him into a coward or allow other hustlers make him fearful of running drugs on their blocks. Time and time again he'd been clear that my mom, me, and now Benzie were the only beings he truly cared about.

Unlike my attitude toward Trinity, me and my dad's relationship wasn't based on hormonal mood swings. I admired my father and was truly a daddy's girl. With him, I was always able to get my way or get myself up out of a punishment I really deserved.

"Yup, you know I am, Daddy. The more product you move, the more money you bring in and can splurge on my birthday gifts." I gave him a big hug and kiss on his cheek. I was a daddy's girl, and everybody knew it.

"You too, Goddaddy. Let me know if I need to give you a list of things I like."

He laughed. "Naw, goddaughter, I don't need a list. I'ma put a few bills in ya hand to set you straight, though. I swear, whatever nigga that you be with better have some long money and deep pockets," he joked seriously.

"You damn right, nigga. Whatever muthafucka I *let* roll with my baby better be coming with more than that." My dad jumped back into the conversation. "We ain't playing with no lightweights. Ain't that right, Porsha?"

I giggled. "Yeah, Daddy. That's right. Let's just drop the topic on me and boys because I know where it can lead," I pleaded.

"We can drop it as long as you know I ain't gonna be on laughing shit if you come up in here otherwise."

I shook my head, rolled my eyes, and took a deep breath, biting my tongue. Both of my parents seemed to be on one today.

My dad continued cooking up while my godfather broke the rocks down. It was usually me, my mom, or sometimes Fame's first baby momma whenever he and she were on the ups, packaging up the product, but I was solo-dolo today. It was cool, though. I'd been taught how to run every position like a boss—even the chef. My dad schooled both me and my mom on how to feed fiends, so we'd never go broke. I packaged product better than I completed schoolwork.

I caught my dad smiling off and on at me for making him proud. I acted like I didn't see him, but I was smiling on the inside. I loved making ole Calvin happy. I was a daddy's girl that was following in his footsteps. I was good at what he was good at, and that was hustling. He'd never worked a day in his life; therefore, Cal taught me how to push it to the max the illegal way.

After two hours of making sure the yellow baggies were sealed in bundles of ten and in Ziploc bags of one hundred, I saw the finish line with the last batch being slid my way. I was glad, too. I'd just gotten a text from my best friend, Imani, saying the field by her house was starting to pop. I was so anxious to get my hot ass in the mix that I started fidgeting, fumbling, and fucking up.

Imani lived down the street from the house I grew up in that my father had workers trapping out of and that I sometimes visited behind my father's back. Me and Imani used to ride bikes and jump rope together as li'l tykes. She was my first real friend, but now my one and only. There was a lot of females who didn't like or tolerated me. I was not for everyone. Wasn't supposed to be, but who cares?

The field was actually four lots combined that were previously the homes of some other friends I remembered but hadn't seen in several years. The city knocked the houses down, yet never rebuilt any homes in their spots. That left a large, unfenced field for folks who lived on the block to loiter on. At first, the kids tried making it a big play area for games like tag, red light/green light, and freeze, but they were eventually run off the lot when the trappin' niggas of the hood made it the hangout spot.

Almost every day in spring, summer and fall, the hustlers who sold baggies out of my old house would hang in the common area to smoke, drink, and get into mischief with young girls like myself. The field was like a Disneyland for THOTS, though the only thing to ride on was a dick. I didn't fit in the category of a neighborhood freak, per se, but I could be a little dehydrated at times— or a lot. I was crushing hard for a nigga named Street.

Street was twenty-four, a certified thug, and reckless as fuck. His name fit him perfectly with his roughneck ass. He was gritty and straight gutta, just how I liked 'em. Day in and out, he hustled hella weight for my dad that helped feed my family. He moved more weight and made more pickups from here than any other dough boy from this hood. Calvin stayed bragging about Street's creds, labeling him a lionhearted moneymaker. My dad might've preached he wanted a different type of man for me, but all I honed in on were Street's thug accolades.

"Daddy, can I go over Imani's house after I give the last runner his package?" I lied, knowing the truth wouldn't get me free. My dad would clown hard if he knew I was one of the fast-tailed girls he talked badly about.

"Yeah, but be home by nine o'clock. You've gotta watch Benzie tonight when me and ya momma go out. Oh, and before I forget, yo' ass is going to school come Monday. I'm tired of that damn attendance officer leaving me voicemails. They left one saying a home visit was next if your attendance didn't improve. And you already know I ain't having no type of ma'fucka poking around my house."

I rolled my eyes, sick of school altogether. I couldn't wait to walk the stage. "Okay, Daddy. I'll be back by nine and then up bright and early on Monday morning for torture. I'll even get the homework they gave in school from Imani when I go over there to get it done over the weekend. I'll play their little game since there's only a month left."

"Yeah, make sure that you do, Porsha. I mean these words, so you better be listening. Me and ya momma both got high school diplomas, and you're not about to fuck up the family tradition by not graduating. Getting a GED is a great achievement, and I'm not discrediting that, but do what you have to do to graduate. Are we speaking the same language?"

"Verbatim," I answered.

I wasn't complying to shut him up. I actually wanted a diploma, even though all the pomp and circumstance along with graduation didn't matter at all. I was more concerned with my birthday that was a week after graduation, which truly symbolized me being grown. A certificate of completion didn't mean you were an adult, but the age on your birth certificate. If I were eighteen now, I wouldn't be having to lie my way up outta there.

Right when I leaped up from my seat, ready to break from the basement, my hopes of leaving sank at the sight of Trinity stumbling in with her glass of liquor. I froze dead in my tracks, thinking she must have the house bugged with cameras and listening devices to always show up right on time.

No one's timing can be this damn perfect.

"Where do you think you're about to sneak off to?" she questioned with her hand on her hip.

"Dad said I could go to Imani's." I threw him under the bus, trying to divert her attention from me to him.

She looked at him then back at me. "Naw, I don't think so. You can dead that plan. We're about to go on a mother/daughter date to the mall and out to eat. Then I need you to do my hair so I can be cute for the cabaret me and your dad are going to tonight."

I tried my best at hiding my disdain while being respectful. I didn't want no parts of a mother/daughter date after how she'd slapped me up earlier.

"Dang, Ma, can I go over Imani's for at least an hour? I'm not just trying to hang with my girl, but find out what I missed in school as well," I begged and lied all at the same time, pulling at strings. I wanted to see the boy I'd been crushing on hard.

"Get the hell out of here, Porsha. I must look like boo-boo the fool or some shit to you," she responded in reference to me mentioning school. "Please don't make me think we're revisiting the same problem I told you not to muthafuckin' revisit. I'll be mad as hell if I've gotta waste my good liquor by tossing it in ya face."

Tensing back up, I recognized her stance as the same one in my bedroom and quickly backed down. Seeing Imani or my crush wasn't worth the beatdown.

"No-no-no-no! We're good. I'll go get dressed." I dropped the shenanigans.

"That'll work. I'll be ready when you are."

"I swear I can't wait until my birthday," I mumbled with my head down, walking out the door.

"What did you say?" she called out, able to hear a ghost blow through the room.

"Nothing. I was just singing a song." I played it off, knowing she knew better but was letting me slide.

Once I was on the other side of the door, I slammed it.

"Calvin, ya better get ya daughter. The li'l heifer thinks I'm playing." I heard her jump on my dad's back about me.

"I swear she gets on my last. Motherfucking. Nerve." I enunciated each syllable as I stomped up the stairs.

Chapter 3

Trinity

"Whatever the fuck ever, Cal. I'm not doing nothing but making that girl show me some respect. I know how I was with my momma once I found out she wasn't gonna put her hands on me for real, and I won't be going through that same bullshit with Porsha." I justified my behavior, trying to outsmart karma. "You can be all buddy-buddy with her if you want."

He raised his hands up and surrendered. "Yeah, whatever. If you're bringing up ya momma, I see you're already on another level. I'ma fall back and keep my peace before we end up getting into it. That's between you and your daughter."

"Yup, you're right. That's why I didn't ask for your opinion in the first place," I snapped, having to have more than the last word.

Calvin's head popped up like one of Benzie's jack-in-the-box toys. Time and time again, he'd told me not to disrespect him, yet once again, I came up outta my bag with some slick shit to say. Even after he'd bowed out.

Chapter 4

Calvin

Before I could catch myself, I leaped up and snatched Trinity by the arm and dragged her into the hallway, pressing her firmly against the wall. "Look, on the real, I suggest you take your ass to the mall or wherever it is you're about to drag Porsha off to and stop trying to get with me. I might let you think you run shit around here, but you don't."

"Are you crazy or high off ya own supply? I know your hands aren't on me."

"You see what's up. Quit tripping." I tightened then loosened my grip, still pushing my weight into her.

"What I see is a crazy nigga that better back up off me so he don't have to sleep light later." She yanked away from me. "And just for you slippin', I'll be taking the whole stash bag from last night."

Watching her ass shake in the too-small shorts she was wearing, I grabbed at my bouncing dick, wishing I could control her feisty ass with it right quick.

Chapter 5

Porsha

"Damn, P! What's taking you so long to pull up over here?" Imani called while I was looking through my dresser drawers for something to jump fresh in real quick.

I smacked my lips as I pulled out a pair of high-waisted ripped jeans. "Girrrl, it's been a change of plans. Trinity is up to her usual hating. She's going somewhere, and I've gotta tag along. I swear to God I can't stand her bipolar behind." I cupped the phone to make sure my conversation stayed private.

"Aww, damn!" Imani was disappointed. "You can't get your dad to get you out of it?"

"Nope, not this time. But I wish I could. Street hasn't hit me up all day. Is here around there?" I was kinda hoping Imani would say no, but she didn't.

"Yeah. He was on the porch with Pete and Dantez."

"There wasn't no girls over there, were there?"

"Girl, bye! Naw! You know I would've told you that as soon as you answered the phone." Imani wasn't lying.

If Street did something in her eyesight, Imani was telling it in detail. I'd caught that nigga up in about ten lies that month alone based on her recall/retell of the situation. I'd come to the conclusion that Street was going to be Street, and that simply meant he was going to do what he wanted to do.

"Okay, well, hit me up if you see him up in a trick's face." I started rushing her off the phone so I could get dressed before my momma barged back into my room.

It didn't take me long to jump fresh. I kept it cute and simple in a pair of ripped jeans, a white tee, and boat shoes. My outfit matched the weather perfectly, plus it was fly enough to rock just in case I got back in time to go over to Imani's.

I could barely get dressed from her blowing my phone up over and over again with picture mail and messages. Super salty over how live it looked around her way, I temporarily sent all her calls to my block box to keep from out my feelings. Graduation and my birthday weren't coming quickly enough.

Trinity swore she'd only be five minutes, but I wasn't betting on it. I opened my Kindle application to pass the time. I'd been reading urban fiction ever since I saw an Instagram post on a blog site hyping up a few titles. After reading one story about chicks from the hood, I'd been hooked. If I could take my ass to school more often, not clown while I was there, and grasp English, I'd be a shoo-in to write a novel. Without a doubt, I was sure my story would sell millions. I'd been through just as much drama as many of the characters I read about, if not more.

Even though the book was hella good, I couldn't get off into it because my mind was too wrapped up in thinking about how I was going to spend the money my dad gave me. He'd filled my hand with bills to spend at the mall as a pre-gift for my birthday. I was happy to have the extra chicken, but he better be coming with more when the actual day arrived. I didn't care that I was running around there screaming grown. He and Trinity better have at least a parting gift for their only daughter.

Shocking me, my mom was true to her word and ready to rock and roll in five minutes. She was dressed in a Victoria's Secret jogging suit, boat shoes, and draped in gold. Unlike a lot of the raggedy, no-style-having mammies around there that wore pajamas all day, mine was a true diva. Everyone on the outside looking in could tell she had chedda, or unlimited access to someone that had it.

After putting her red cup of juice and alcohol into the cup holder, she tossed her oversized purse into the back seat. Calvin must've broken her off with way more money than me. I was not hating, though. I was happy with what I had, plus I knew there was more coming with my birthday being only weeks away. Calvin spoiled both of us without questions asked. Quiet as it's kept, I hoped he continued that pattern with me even after I was up and out of the house—especially since I also hoped he provided and furnished me with a place.

I low key had my eye on this unit a few blocks away. It was close enough for me to have my parents' protection, yet far enough for me to have privacy.

"I hope you've got your charger," my mom said, plugging her phone in.

"Yup, it's right here." I dangled it, then buckled up in the passenger seat of her Ram 150. My mom didn't believe in tiny cars. She claimed you can't do damage in 'em. Every vehicle she owned had been a truck sitting on rims. I wanted my first whip, however, to be a cute foreign car.

Turning her sound system up, N.W.A.'s "Fuck the Police" poured out of the speakers. Trinity always flossed hard with the sounds on bang and the windows down. I didn't know why she bothered rolling them down since people couldn't see us for how fast she drove. My hair was blowing in the wind as she bent corners to the freeway. We were headed out to eat first.